I0772714

I've Always Loved

B.A. McRae

Content & Trigger Warning

|| severe anxiety || || toxic relationship || || grief || mentions of blood ||

|| suicide || || self-harm || || PTSD || brief gun usage ||

Within this story are sensitive topics that could potentially cause discomfort and or stress to some readers.

As an author who cares about their readers, I wanted to make these clear, and express that the topics mentioned above are not and should not be romanticized.

Humanity suffers and struggles with a multitude of hardships, let's always remember to be kind, because you never know what someone may be going through.

1. 

2.

3.

4.

5.

6.

7.

8.

9.

10.

11. 

12.

13.

14.

15.

16.

17.

18.

19.

20.

21. 

22.

23.

1. Epic

Five o'clock in the damn morning; I haven't been up this early since my days at the nursing home. And since I had arisen so early, I decided wholeheartedly that I deserved some exceptional coffee.

Or, yes, okay, busted. I just need an extra shot of espresso or something to wake me up.

The brisk morning wind makes me feel a bit tense instead of awake. Woah, hold it, I just thought of something. What if the morning wind is equivalent to the morning's breath? That's kind of mind-blowing, taking morning breath to a whole other level.

Goodness gracious, I need coffee *now*.

The past few days have been interestingly hectic. Though Jude and Carder were stoked that I agreed to go to Julia's wedding, and I can't deny I have a bit of excitement, I still feel uneasy about the whole thing.

We agreed on driving instead of flying; that was mostly on me. I'm already jumpin' outta the only place I've ever known. I'm not about to soar the air on the same day; baby steps. Plus, it's not *that* bad. It's roughly a seven-hour drive, and with each of us pitching in twenty-five dollars for gas, we should be golden.

Carder and I negotiated with Alan that we would work regular shop hours and begin to pack away the majority of the books. Alan has been off ordering and organizing new things for the renovations he has in mind for the past two days. As far as I know, this will be done while we're gone.

'Books & Such will revolutionize all small business bookstores everywhere. It's a hero, it's an inspiration, it's the future!' as Alan puts it.

The brief walk to the coffee shop went quickly, with the assistance of inner haunting thoughts produced by lack-of-coffee withdrawals and the anticipation of being greeted with that scented wall of coffee beans, chocolate croissants, and vanilla.

I ordered honey lattes for myself, Carder, and Jude, to get a spring in our step before the big journey, but before I took off on my walk back, I needed to phone a friend.

Taking a seat at a table near the window with my caffeinated company, I scrolled through my contact list. And only a few short rings later, the sigh of relief released from my anxious shell of an existence.

"Well, hello there, my Dear Traveler! It is mighty early!"

This call has been a second long, and I already feel a bit better. "Well, hello there, my Dear Father." I kept my giggle at a minimum, slightly getting down to business. "Are you busy at the moment? Would it be okay if I talked to you about something?"

"Of course, Traveler. Would you like mom to weigh in on this convo?"

I adore his usage of lingo. "I would love to talk to you and mom in a moment, but just you and I can talk right now if that's alright. If you want to fill in mom later, that's okay with me. I just wanted to talk to you right now."

As if we were in the same room, I felt his vibe switch from the goofy-silly pops to the dad who came in with the superhero cape to pick me up from school after my first anxiety scene.

"I'm all ears; whelp, not literally. You might have turned out a little weird if half your genetics were ears."

Well, we couldn't expect the goofy part of dad to completely shut off. "You certainly got me there. I am thankful for our normal ear ratio." We shared a short laugh as I then cleared my throat. But I guess I wasn't ready to start the conversation.

"So," Dad took a deep breath. "Today is the big day, huh?"

"Why yes, it is. Today we leave; tomorrow is the wedding, and to be honest, I'm not really sure what we have planned after that."

It sounded like he was maneuvering around the kitchen, probably searching for his favorite mug and a stirring spoon. "And let's do a check-in. How do you feel about all of this?"

Taking a shallow breath, even though I needed a deeper one, I felt a little nervous leading into this topic. It's the whole purpose of the phone call, but still.

"I'm excited, really I am. To see what's beyond the city limits of Virginia Beach. And to be doing it with Carder and Jude, but," Trailing off, I could feel my chest let out a warning of tightness.

"I can't imagine the tumbles of emotions you've been carrying with you for the past few days, and today especially. What you're embarking on doing is one of the largest leaps you've taken in life. Does it make you feel better to do it with Carder and Jude?"

Dad's always been so perceptive of how I'm feeling. Both my parents are, but dad, just kind of, gets it more.

"Yea, I feel really supported by both of them. And they've never made me feel bad for the fears I have. They just automatically accepted me for who I am. I feel safe, I guess, taking this step with them."

"There's a Beatles lyric I'm reminded of," He cleared his throat.

At the same time, I sightly giggled along with a playful eye roll waiting for his lyric annotation.

"It's simple, as most of their profound lyrics are, but it rings true. *'I get by with a little help from my friends'*. I'm not always the person who believes everything happens for a reason. Still, I feel that these two people in your life have wandered onto your path for a reason, Traveler."

I expected that lyric to come up, though it was still nice to hear the words in his voice. But I was not expecting to receive his following sentiment, which made me curious to hear more. "Could you unpack that, please?"

"Oh yea, just a sec. Let me get situated in my porch chair."

I could hear a little muffle and the creak of old craftsmanship wood before he returned to our conversation, which now had a dash of philosophi-calness.

"So, unpacking what I said. I think people intertwine in each other's paths for a reason. Some help us continue onto our own path as they wave goodbye and pick back up on theirs, or you create a whole new one for the both of you. Either way, when we allow people to get close to us, it's usually because we can feel that they have something enriching to bring to our life. And vice versa."

The chair's creaking now had a rhythm; he was rocking and lecturing. Whatta guy.

"That's just what I think, but I was an art professor, not an anthropology professor. So I guess you can take my words as you'd like."

I've never *not* thought my dad was intelligent and wise, but holy buckets, I don't think I've been giving him enough credit.

"That was some pretty deep stuff, dad. Thank you for that." Taking in an inhale, I formulated my next question for this long-distance lecture.

"So, you think Carder and Jude are my path people?"

"Lucy," There was a smidge of comedy and up-frontness in his tone. "I think we both know they are your path people."

Rarely do I hear him call me by my name. It's usually Traveler, or when Colin and I were kids, he'd call us by random Beatles member names or names mentioned in Beatles songs. My favorite that I can recall is being referred to as Sgt. Pepper.

"I think you're right; I feel very close to them. I'm just scared. I'm terrified of leaving, of letting the world outside my comforting, familiar walls become a part of me. I don't know if I want it to. I don't want to disappoint Carder, Jude, or you and mom. I don't know if I want to do this anymore."

I released a breath, and with it was a weight dropped off from finally letting out some raw thoughts. I'm usually one to beat around the bush until someone gets the core truth out of me, but I just needed to let it go this time.

"Then don't."

"Wait, what?"

"Don't go." He repeated as I heard him nonchalantly sip on his coffee. "If you don't want to go, then don't."

"But I do," Hearing his response made me feel uncharacteristically defensive. "I want to go."

"I thought you didn't want to go anymore?"

Sighing, I shrugged my shoulders, "Who knows what I want anymore."

Dad took a calming breath, which prompted me to do the same, and we both exhaled around the same time. "If you'd like to know what I think, I think you should go, and I think Jude and Carder are the perfect people to accompany you on this journey. There are things you should and are meant to experience. Amazing, life-changing things! You have yet to find pieces of yourself waiting to be picked up by you."

"I did want to know what you thought. That's honestly why I called. You always know what to say." I paused, searching for any other hidden feelings I needed to release. And as it turns out, there was one left.

"But what if it turns out bad? And it's not all that it was cut out to be?"

He took a moment to answer this one. "Then you come back home, and you don't leave again if it doesn't feel right. But you live knowing you tried. Truthfully, I don't think you're afraid of it going poorly, Traveler." Dad sipped on his coffee once more, like he was taking notes from Carder on how to make a dramatic delivery. "I think you're afraid you'll like it."

Alright, dad, way to hit me with the big wave of holy moly. "Are you sure you didn't study the fine arts of *mindblowing*?"

"You don't have to study what you're naturally gifted with." We both laughed together, and it felt like a fitting seal for that conversation.

"You got me there. Hey, is it okay if I put my headphones in so I can talk to you and mom while I walk back to my apartment? Could you get mom, please?"

Of course, dad obliged, and I set my phone down and untangled my headphones before plugging them in. I couldn't shake his last sentence out of my head. Maybe talking with both of them will help my mind settle into a good place before returning to Carder and Jude.

With my headphones in, my phone chilling out in my back pocket, and a drink carrier of lattes in my hands, I returned to the phone call. "Hey, dad, mom, are you there?"

"Lucy! Lucy Lucy Lucy, it's today! Right? Right, it's today, isn't it?"

Mom is still getting the hang of volume control when it comes to speaking on the phone, but her excitement made me feel, well, kinda proud of myself.

"Yes, Dear, it's today. Today is the day our Traveler embarks on her new adventure, taking the world by storm!"

"We are both so proud, Lucy; we love you so much. This is such a big step."

Ya know, I'm happy, really I am. I can feel my face radiating in a way it only could when I hear that both my parents are proud of me. And although it feels good overall, I'm still a bit overwhelmed by the situation. "Thank you, Mom, thank you, Dad, that means the world to me."

Walking with the morning air of Virginia Beach felt gentle and comforting. The only morning air I've ever experienced; I know it well. And I swear it was filling me with a feeling, a message. A message that it was okay to go, and perhaps I should.

"I just wanted to call you guys before we headed out, which will be soon, according to the Carder Itinerary. We leave at six-thirty, and I didn't pack yet. I've been pushing it off."

Okay, first off, the farthest I've ever gone to stay overnight somewhere was probably Carder's Aunt's house at the far end of town. So this whole packing thing is new territory to me; the only actual packing I've done is moving from the family house to my apartment. And that doesn't count because everything had to go. Lastly, I don't know the first thing about what to wear to a wedding or even what to wear in New York City. Why can't I just live in an Audrey Hepburn movie, and this would all be embedded character knowledge? Okay, wait a moment to appreciate the greatness that is Audrey Hepburn. Thank you; on we go.

Dad chimed into my Audrey-filled thoughts. "Well, we won't keep you on the phone too long then, and don't worry champ, packing isn't as scary as you think."

I could hear the backhanded slap on the arm mom gave him. I liked his humor, though.

"We love you, Lucy, so so so much. Please check in, okay? Please?"

Oh, mother, "Yes, mom, of course, I love you guys so so so much too!"

I loved that feeling; that mutual unspoken feeling when you can, in a sense, hear the other person's smile. Gosh, I love it. "I'll call you guys soo-"

"Oh! And take lots of pictures! And, and make sure Carder watches out for you so you don't get lost. Hold hands if you need to. I know he won't mind-"

"Dear lord, please, it's too early for your theories." Dad humorously interrupted.

"Tucker, they are not theories. I know it, you know it, and Carder obviously knows it."

I decided to intervene before this became a deep dive into mom's thoughts on Carder and me. "Okay, well, on that note, I should probably get goin' happy couple." Surprisingly Mom laughed along with that one. "I love you, Mom; I love you, Dad."

"I love you honey, please, please be safe." Mom made the sound she would have made had she been here to kiss me on the forehead, and I'm guessing she went somewhere private to keep from crying. That was just kind of mom's thing to do.

I heard dad return to his outside chair. "Hey, don't go changing on me in that big city, alright?"

"Wouldn't dream of it." Chuckling softly from my exhale.

"Talk to you soon, Traveler. I love you."

"Wait! Wait, wait, Dad?"

"Yes, yes, I'm still on the line."

On the line. Oh dad, I love ya. "Take Mom out on a fun night, something spontaneous and exciting." There was the lovely smiling feeling again.

"What a fine idea; it will be epic!"

"Goodness gracious," I couldn't control my laugh for a second there. "I didn't even know you knew that word, let alone used it." After we joined in a second of laughter, we finally returned to our goodbye. "You have an epic time, dad."

"And you have an epic trip, Traveler."

As I continued my walk through the modest crowd of sidewalk people to return to my modest apartment with my not-so-modest but no doubt wonderful best friend, I can honestly say I felt better than before. And upon arriving at my destination, it was confirmed that I could do this.

And apparently, Alan was helping us too; as I was surprised to see him carrying what I could tell was Carder's luggage into Carder's car. Alan also had Carder's Broadway lanyard, which he insisted on buying just for this trip, clenched between his teeth. I saw the look of panic settle in his eyes while opening the door. A man can only carry so much unnecessary over-packing baggage.

I ran over just when one of the suitcases slipped out of his grip and caught it before hitting the ground. Yes, with one hand, somehow keeping latte balance and the other catching a hefty bag. How in the world was it accomplished? I have no clue. And for that, yes, indeed, I deserve this: Point for Lucy.

Letting the bag gently go and setting the drink carrier over on the roof of Carder's car, I came back to pick up the heavy suitcase I had caught so badassly.

With his now free hand, he set his teeth free. "Oh, thank you, thank you, Lucy." Both of us walked over to the car; I made my way to the back as he popped the trunk. "Excited about your trip?"

"Ye-"Beginning to lift the suitcase, "Holy Bucke-"I was literally breaking a sweat trying to get this thing in there. I think I toned my arms by the time I slammed it in the trunk. "How much stuff does he need?"

And but of course, there the Queen appeared like he knew we were talking about him. "Lucy, it is way too early for this kind of sass; meet me halfway."

Rolling my eyes to see he had another overnight bag in his grip. "Yea, yea, okay, I gotta pack quick before Jude gets here-"

At the sound of Carder throwing, yes literally throwing, the apparent light bag in the trunk with the rest of his bags, he cut me off. "Already done, you're welcome, please just," Goodness gracious, he looked like hell. Well, the lovely side of it. You know, hell's good side. "I'm dying; please be a saint and hand me a latte."

My eyebrows rose, as did the side of my lips, turning into a slight smirk. "Oh, a latte? You mean one of these little lattes?"

"Lucy, I swear."

"I could have sworn, looking back into the book of Carder quotes I keep handy in my mind-"

"You're a creep."

"My name is Carder, and I would rather wear velvet tracksuits the rest of my life than drink a latte earlier than 9am."

Before Carder shot him a death glare, Alan was laughing at my, might I say, spot-on impression.

"First off," Carder put up a finger. "My voice is deeper than that. Second off, Alan just stop."

Alan turned to me as I had the same look of puzzlement on my face as he did. Alan turned back to Carder as he was about to, I assume, ask what Carder was referring to.

"Stop being so, Alan. Lastly, Lucy, I will die from lack of sleep in a prison cell because I am about to murder everyone within a ten-mile radius if I don't get some caffeine in me. For the sake of humanity, please. Give me the bean juice."

I turned to Alan to see him holding his composure. "As you can see, Alan, Carder is very much a morning person." Ah, there we go; I got a little smile out of Alan and a sassy half-smile out of Carder.

While the two began rearranging the luggage in the trunk, I left two lattes in the drink carrier and took one with me. I then went inside to get the bag that Carder apparently packed for me.

Strolling down to my room, I saw my new suitcase packed, zipped, and ready to go. What would I do without this guy? Actually, I'm pretty impressed; he had to have packed that bag fairly quick while I was out getting our morning drinks and talking to mom and dad. Some of me was curious about what he packed, but another part was relieved I didn't have to do it myself.

I could hear the front door open and light, sleepy footsteps make their way into my room; but my eyes were fastened to my bag. Why? I don't know; it's morning. Give me a break.

Breaking my stare appeared Carder's arm, reaching for my bag to bring downstairs.

"Carder, I can take my own bag; it's alright." As I went to grab the handle, he snatched it away.

"No," Pulling the adjustable handle up and propping the bag on its two back wheels. "I packed it."

It doesn't even matter if Carder is not a morning person, "So, therefore, I should carry it down since you went through the trouble already." He is always a stubborn person.

With a mischievous grin, he responded: "*I* packed it, so, therefore, there's roughly four hundred pounds worth of clothes in here."

Rolling my eyes, I gave him an exaggerated sigh.

"Thank you for the lovely drink Lucy-Lou."

Alas, he knows I can't be mad at him when he calls me that; how could I? It sounds like something out of a Dr. Seuss book. "Oh, and Jude pulled in about two minutes ago. He and Alan are talking about who knows what."

Internally I laughed at the image of Jude and Alan having a heart-to-heart.

Carder and I were about to walk out the apartment door when it was abruptly opened, just as I was going to turn the knob. Luckily with my ninja moves, I didn't get hit by the door.

"Goodness! I'm sorry!" Alan quickly apologized as he and Jude came in. "Did I hit you?"

Smiling to reassure him, I shook my head. "No, don't worry, I'm fine. Thank you, by the way, for helping us, Alan. I didn't even know you were coming over!"

"Well, of course I would come and help my favorite employees! Regardless of the number of employees I actually have."

Two. I'm pretty sure Alan just has the two.

I gave him a smile despite the laughter in a lump in my throat. "I'm sorry I would have brought a latte for you had I known you'd be here." I felt pretty guilty for not having some kind of gratitude in drink form for him.

"Oh heavens, it's really no trouble to trifle over. I am excellent." Alan responded in his classic matter-of-fact yet nonsensical tone.

My eyes drifted to that messy strawberry blonde hair, and now my mind was also a mess- I lost my train of thought. Superman has his kryptonite, and I, my soft tousled haired men. Hot damn, back on track.

"There's a latte for you in the drink carrier downstairs, Mr. Johnson." Add his dorky morning smile to the weakness list; that just nearly killed me.

"Why, thank you so very much, *Mrs. Cumberbatch.* I look forward to trying it!" After addressing me, he turned to Carder with the same smile. "And it is always a pleasure to see you, Mr. Fashion."

Surprisingly, I thought Carder would have torn that nickname apart, but he laughed and gave Jude a fist-bump.

With that, Jude and Alan took a break at our fine little table while Carder and I walked down the apartment stairs to put my bag in the car. Holding the door open for him just as we both had stepped outside, Carder lost it.

And by it, I mean his shit. Carder lost his shit. As I did, too. Just quieter and to myself. What in the he-

"WHAT THE HELL!" Carder bewilderedly shouted with rage. After he cut his scream off, he ditched the suitcase and bolted for his car.

Rescuing yet another bag from hitting the ground, I hurried over, wheeling the suitcase behind me. Good lord, Carder wasn't joking; this bag is 400 pounds too heavy.

As I approached the car, I hoped my eyes were mistaken about what they saw after opening the apartment building door. But my eyesight is fine; Carder's tires have been unmercifully slashed.

Both our jaws dropped. The only difference was Carder's spewing out angry words straight from the depths of his soul that had not yet been treated with coffee, as mine was dried up from puzzlement.

"What, WHY, why, who, what in the HELL! Damnit! Who would-"

We both recognized a face walking towards the apartment building and tried to ignore the scene.

"Wait, Lucy, that's the old lady who lives on the second floor,"

Yes, I remember. "Yea, but Card-" I also remember how much she hates us.

"Ma'am! Excuse me!" He politely called out to the second-floor tenant. "Someone slashed my tires; it must have happened within the last five minutes or so. Did you see who did it? Please, it's important; we're about to go-"

"Damn you!" As she shook her veiny fist at us, I think that ought to have jogged his memory of why this lady never talked to us.

Before we discovered she was a total jerk who was very vocal about her disapproval of Carder's, in her words, "lifestyle", she looked like a sweet old lady. Like the one you would see in some heartwarming film about *the true meaning of family* or an old Christmas classic. But no, this slightly hunched over, tiny, hoarse-voiced chick would be staring in a short film titled *The Lost Hope of Humanity*.

"Oh, get over it, lady! And get some therapy!" Yepp, by the irritated tone in his voice and the blood rushing to his cheeks, he certainly remembers her now.

Boy, did that comeback kick her pacemaker up a notch. "Go to hell!" I'm surprised how loudly she yelled that it didn't knock the wind right out of her.

"Yea?! Well, save me a spot for bingo once you get there!"

Snaps! I didn't even give a second thought to our situation as I gave Carder a high five. That was one hell of a good comeback; it was so natural! The mic fricken dropped, and without another word, his cranky homophobic competitor shuffled away.

But sadly, we were still left with four slashed tires. And no explanation.

"Well, this is some shit, everything was going just dandy up until this fiasco, and that old hag was just the flippin' cherry on top!"

I was going to place a hand on his shoulder to calm him down, but I felt he would probably just get more wound up.

"I'm going to flip shit, I can't- Can you please stay by the car while I go up and get Jude and Alan?"

Without a reply, Carder, with now an actual reason, dramatically left the scene. What more would I expect, though? That soul was born into this world with a stage filter over his eyes.

But seriously, what would drive someone to do this?

I walked over and grabbed the last latte off the car; surprisingly, it wasn't spilled. Taking a lap around the vehicle to see if any other damage was done, I stopped on the other side.

I swear something caught the corner of my eye from the back tire. Curiously I kneeled down to see that my assumption, and once again my eyesight, was on point.

Within the tire cut, I could see something thin and white stuffed between the rubber. Setting the latte down next to me, I carefully pulled out the mysterious item with the tips of my pointer finger and thumbnail. Though I felt like fricken *Sherlock Holmes* at the moment, I instantly felt my stomach shoot its way up into my throat as my pupils dilated at the sight of it in my palm.

I heard the building door close, and Carder angrily filled in Jude and Alan. I pocketed the evidence, stood up, and made my way to the front of the car with my latte in hand before the gents even noticed me.

"Gezz, who would even do this? And to each tire, that's some dedication right there." Jude sounded more impressed than upset as Carder gave him a glare.

"We are going to fall behind schedule, and then the whole day will be thrown off, all because of some fricken idiot who decided to go on a stabbing spree."

"Okay, okay, we're going to fix this. Don't worry. We are going to get back on schedule; I'm determined." Although Jude's award-winning reassuring smile didn't wholly help with Carder's scarily calm kept rage, it still lightened the vibe.

"How about this, we take my Jeep, and I'll help you get new tires when we return from our trip?"

It looked like Carder's arms would lose circulation from how tightly crossed they were. After he let out a sigh, they loosened a bit. "Yes, and thank you to the Jeep offer and no to the tires. That's not your fault; that's some psychopath's fault. I'm not making you pay for that."

Excitingly Jude responded, "Yes! We are a go! And the tires weren't negotiable; it's happening." This fella made one of the boldest moves I think I've ever seen, Carder-wise. He tousled Carder's hair and started unloading the trunk.

I'm sorry; let me just repeat that.

HE TOUSLED CARDER'S HAIR.

Carder, the guy who doesn't stop fixing his hair until every single piece is in its rightful place. That's like throwing ice at Satan. Okay, wow, I don't know why that just popped up in my head. But now I can't help but imagine goony little Jude holding an ice cube tray in one hand and releasing a handful of ice from the other at this ginormous beast. Goodness, I need help.

After packing almost the whole backseat full of luggage, you can only imagine who took up the most space, Carder and I decided to alternate seats between stops along the way.

Shortly after we arranged the bags, so they weren't in Jude's way of seeing out the back, I heard Alan reassure Jude that he would check on Tom while we were gone. That's what they must have been talking about while Carder and I were occupied.

And then, Alan bid me and Carder farewell and informed us that the shop would miss us deeply.

Oh Alan, never stop being so, well, as Carder puts it, Alan.

It felt so strange unplugging everything, turning off all the lights, and, lastly, shutting and locking the door; it sounded odd and stupid, but this was new to me. The longest I had ever been away from home was probably no more than a couple of days. Still, it didn't scare me or make me homesick because home was always a phone call or bike ride away.

And now, I'll be roughly 350 miles away. Thank you, Google Maps.

Now that I think about it, there's no one to call home to. But I don't really want to think about it. I want to take a deep breath and say something cool to myself.

Like: *This is it, MacArthur.*

Climbing into the back, I pulled my legs up into a criss-cross position because some bags were where my feet would rest. I took another deep breath and finally started to process in my mind how crazy this all was.

The three of us are on a road trip to one the biggest and busiest cities in the U.S. This is definitely a milestone within our friendships. One that came pretty quick and one that's a bit overdue.

Carder and Jude were discussing music choices. Which shortly turned into a back-and-forth lecture on how none of the cassettes are appropriately labeled. Which ultimately ended with a rundown on the directions we were going to take to get out of town.

During all of that oh-so-exciting conversation, my mind was lost and tangled in snippets of memories.

The still moments with mom showing kindness and attention to the most minor details that I would have never noticed and taken for granted had it not been for her. Jam sessions with dad and dance parties with grandpa. Late nights under the boardwalk lights that make you forget how dark it got when you first got there. Picture perfect moments of running barefoot on the beach with Col-

Colin.

Colin would have loved this idea.

I could move over the suitcase next to me just enough for him to have a seat.

We would have enough room.

We have enough room.

My mind made a full circle in the fast slideshow of these moments; I had never put together or thought about it really that I was about to make a memory that wasn't within the city limits of Virginia Beach.

I was about to journey off from the only place I had ever known. About to say goodbye to my city.

Oh, let's not pull a Carder here and be so melodramatic; this isn't a goodbye. This is nothing more than a see you later.

I guess I was spacing out as my eyes came back into focus to see Carder and Jude smiling at me.

Carder reached out to my hand, slipping it into mine and giving it a light squeeze. "Ready, Lucy-Lou?"

My eyes looked at Jude for a moment; inside those grey-blue eyes, I could see a small celebration and exhilaration bursting within his irises. From that, I switched my view to Carder, whom I could tell was excited but trying his best to hide his concern for me. But I didn't want him to worry. I wanted him to be happy and to have the time of his life during this trip.

All of our smiles reflected the same broad, radiantly blissful shine as I answered Carder's question with a soft squeeze of his hand. Our secret language. After releasing his hand, Carder turned and nodded to Jude like he was reporting to his captain. Carder pushed in a cassette tape with a vibrant pink tape label. I'm guessing they tried to compromise, but Carder won. The Queen never loses.

But I must say, though he probably didn't know what would pop up on the cassette, it was very fitting. And I loved how right when that first note hit the speakers, we all perked up and motioned to turn it up.

I'm never one for a full blast, but there was no way this shit wasn't getting blasted. Might I just say that we, right now, are the coolest people about to road trip in style.

The top is off, and the weather is a perfect seventy-five degrees with just a tiny amount of wind. And streaming out of the speakers and into the rushing atmosphere, through the strands of my hair dancing with the wind as we raced through traffic, was 'Send Me on My Way' by Rusted Root.

It couldn't have been more perfect. Even though the chorus was pretty much the only part we could sing with 100% confidence, we sang it loud and proud to all the passing cars, right up to where I could see the city limits sign.

And as the words, send me on my way, repeated themselves and meant something different each time the sentence rang through my ears, I placed my hand on the other seat. I closed my fist tight as we sped past the sign and over the border of Virginia Beach.

Like Colin was there, I looked to my side, thinking,

Holy shit, holy shit, we did it! *We did it! We left!*

I swore I could picture him sitting there.

I could see Colin holding my hand; he was just as psyched as me.

As Carder looked back and I turned to him just in time to catch his reaction, I don't think he noticed what I was doing or wouldn't care anyway. My gosh, we were like little kindergartners whose crush just shared their animal crackers with us, giggling and giddy. I turned around to look out the back to see what the city looked like from behind me.

Above the music, Jude called to me in an enthusiastic voice. "How does the back of that Virginia Beach sign look, Lucy?"

And as the last notes of our travel song eased and began to fade out, my smile couldn't have been more content at this moment.

And I didn't care if either of them saw me reach and place my hand on the seat, holding Colin's hand again.

Clearing my throat as a small chuckle only I could hear escaped off my vocal cords, I answered in a tone of my voice I'd never heard before. "It feels epic."

2. The Musical Jeep 

As the road trip cassette continued, I slouched back, as did Carder's passenger   seat driving. We aren't even an hour out of Virginia Beach, and I'm already about to die of Carder-over-exposure.

Every red light, he wants to run.

If a car in front of us is going slower than Carder would like, let's just say he's already leaned over and honked the horn, I might add, three times.

Seven. Whole. Hours.

How many minutes is that exactly?

Ugh, I hate math with a burning passion.

I can't do this kind of Math in my head-

Lucy.

Duh, phone, calculator.

Thank goodness for this blessed technology I can carry in my pocket.

"Lucy."

Popping my head up while my ears adjusted to the now lower volume to see Carder, with his needy face on. This is somewhat of a rare Carder; it only appears every other crisis a year. We are thankful it isn't a regular occurrence.

With a roll of my eyes, I gave him a slight smirk and looked back down at my phone to continue my quest for curiosity numbers. "Yes, can I help you?"

"Yes." He paused, of course. Always the dramatized pause. "Yes, indeed you can. I'm dangerously bored."

Releasing a sarcastic, maybe just a tad of amusement, sigh as my eyebrow rose with the expectations of this explanation, I decided to entertain this car-theatric domain of his. "Dangerously, huh?"

"Yes, again." He replied, fully engaged in this temporary role of a five-year-old who is experiencing his first long trip in the car. "Pay attention, I need entertainment, or things will get ugly very quickly in this musical Jeep."

Finishing off my equation, I gave him a glare. "Okay, did you know there are four hundred and twenty minutes in seven hours?"

Jude and I made eye contact in the driver's mirror for a moment; I only needed to see his eyes for that long to deduce his cheerful excitement. I could just tell how happy he was that this trip was happening. *Look who's the Sherlock now.*

Casually switching my gaze, I, well, anyone for that matter, could have deduced Carder's sudden burst of adrenaline from finding the solution to his boredom problem.

Throwing his seatbelt off, climbing over the bags and onto the seat next to me, he plopped himself down cross-legged with his seatbelt somehow securely on. I think it's safe to say my assumption is correct. The best part of this abrupt change of scene was Jude's reaction, which was nothing.

"No, I didn't know that; keep going." Carder, facing towards me like we were on our apartment couch, requested with a huge geeky smile on his face. This face of Carder's is not rare, but alas, it is one of my favorites.

"Comeoncomeon, I'm hungry for more interestingly useless facts!"

I didn't move a facial muscle; he knew what he was missing.

"Pretty please?"

Atta Carder.

Though I laughed at his wishes, I, too, had a craving curiosity for odd facts. "Alright, give me a sec." Typing away in the Google search bar. Google, honestly, what a beautiful thing. *God bless Google.*

And so, we scrolled through pages and pages of weird facts:

Fact–You must play ping-pong for twelve hours to lose one pound.

Carder's Reaction (CR, if you will)–*We're investing in a ping-pong table at Books & Such.*

Fact–In a person's average lifetime, they will walk the equivalent of five times around the equator.

CR–*That makes my legs hurt.*

Fact–The state of Florida is bigger than England.

CR–*That makes my brain hurt.*

Fact–Hawaii is the only state that grows coffee.

CR–*Never mind, we'll put off buying a ping-pong table until we have found a local coffee company in Hawaii to purchase our coffee from.*

Fact–Buzz Aldrin was one of the first men on the moon, and his mother's maiden name was also moon.

CR–*Did you make that one up?*

Fact–The average person takes 23,000 breaths a day

CR–*Great, now all I'm going to be able to think of is counting how many times I breathe.*

Then that led to a whole bunch of would you rather questions, for example:

Lucy, would you rather let me pick your outfits for the rest of your life or give up coffee for the rest of your life?

As you can imagine, most of these sounded more like real threats than a game.

But alas, it all spun down to us watching adorably short clips of puppies doing cute little puppy things. I'm not complaining at all. It's a hell of a lot easier and more entertaining. Let's be honest; who doesn't love watching tiny animals make silly mistakes they will have no consequences for? It's adorable.

"Alright, my boredom tank is empty, thank you, I am now going to take my rightful spot." Carder, out of nowhere, nonchalantly said while once again climbing over everything until he was back in the front seat.

And with the newly open space, I moved into the middle seat, clicked the seatbelt on, and made it a tad bit loose, so I could lie down. I closed my eyes and let all the worries get tangled in the wind like my current hair status.

Stretching my legs out as much as I could and laying my head on the seat, I looked at my feet- it made me think about the times my mom and I both laid down on the couch. Each on a different end, and we'd just talk. Gosh, we'd talk for hours and think only thirty minutes had passed. Sometimes we would just talk the crap out of one topic, or a book could have been written on how much would be covered in one couch-talking session.

I remember dad and Colin going for a *boy's night out*. Upon coming back, they found us in the same position, laughing about stupid inside couch jokes and bookmarking in our minds where we left off for the next time.

I miss those talks, the old family house, hell, and even the couch. I'd love to pop up out of nowhere to surprise mom with dad's help, and we could have our couch time again.

We could have a family moment and laugh during dinner. Experiment with mixing different things in our waffle mix. If you haven't tried adding coffee creamer to your waffle batter, I'll say you're welcome in advance.

Honestly, I can't even recall the last dinner we had.

That's kind of odd to think about; when was the last time you did something for the last time. I guess, to some degree, you can't have too much under that category until you've passed away, but it's still something to think about.

With that floating about in my mind, Colin came strolling in, and I thought about all his last times.

The last time he and dad laid on their backs with the turntable in the middle of the living room floor, they *studied* different albums and ranked them from best to worst.

The last time all four of us went out to eat, or five when grandpa was still around.

When was the last time Colin slid down the stair railing and successfully slid off like a badass, and the last time he fell on his ass?

Oh gosh, I don't even think I could guess the last thing we watched together on Netflix.

When was the last time Colin, Carder, and I went to the theater and bawled our eyes out at some movie that probably wasn't intended to be a tear-jerker? Still, we left with runny noses and puffy eyes?

Or the last time we both said the same word at the same time and turned our heads so quickly towards each other with our jaws dropped like we just discovered something veracious that would benefit the world.

The last time we ran on the boardwalk.

I guess the most recently last time we had, was our last game of *Doctor and Companion.*

Still focused on my feet, I pictured he was lying there too, but he wasn't looking at me. He had his hands under his head, eyes closed, a blissful smile across his face, and a soft hum from him underneath the music playing in the Jeep.

I could only imagine the ideas and thoughts that kept Colin busy and the thought-out still frames that glossed the inside of his eyelids. What I wouldn't give to be able to ask him a thousand questions, but they would probably all disappear the instant I saw him.

They would blend into one haunting question: Why did you leave me?

"STOP!" Catching me *completely* off guard, Carder screamed his command.

Jude quickly halted the car, and I gripped the back of the passenger's seat to keep from slamming into the bags. The Jeep pulled the car off to the side of the road.

As I took off my seat belt once we were parked, I gave Carder a confused and startled look. "How long was I spacing out?"

"IRRELEVANT!" Again, he yelled while lashing his arm out, pointing to me like we were about to joust.

I shook my head just a tad out of even more confusion and turned to Jude.

"About two-ish hours, Carder poked you-"

"Yes, yes, I poked you. We have other matters to discuss." Carder looked around, almost in a paranoid way.

Still looking at Jude, we both shrugged and waited for Carder to continue.

"I would like to propose a detour stop to the council."

Just go with it, Lucy. "Where are we?"

With the slight turn of Carder's head towards me, my mood inside shifted. "Dover, Delaware"

"Oh my gosh."

"Wait, what's the significance of Dover?" Jude jumped in.

I was about to explain, but this wasn't my story to tell.

"This, this God-forsaken place, is where I grew up. With my parents. Until they threw me out."

I could see the concern on Jude's face; gosh, I haven't even met Carder's folks, and they make my stomach churn.

"If it pleases the council, I'd like to drive by the old house."

Our council of two nodded in agreement.

"Thank you." Carder slipped his seatbelt back on and now directed the conversation to Jude. "I'll give you directions; it's not too far off our route."

Merging back into traffic, all of us securely in our seats, we started on the side quest of our big adventure.

Mission Uncultured Bastards.

Carder's choice of name. Isn't he just so creative?

After about twenty minutes, the Jeep slowly stopped on the other side of the street of Carder's old house. It was modest and pleasant, like any average American Dream home with the white picket fence and all that junk.

Jude turned the engine off, and we all sat silently, staring at the house like we were on a stakeout. There was a big window in the front of the house; you could perfectly see their kitchen and dining room table.

"George and Margret Elizondo, the assholes of my life. Margret never put curtains on that window. She loved having the neighborhood see her serve dinner on her stupid tacky plate ware, and her makeup, to this day, gives me night terrors. Image. Image is literally all they ever cared about. The yard needed to be greener than everyone else's, our Christmas lights needed to be the brightest, and above all, their son had to live up to their standards."

Carder's eyes became glossy as he stared at the place that I guess never really was home to him. "They didn't live up to mine anyway." Turning to me for just a second, he gave me a smirk, but as his eyes settled back on the house, an expression of disgust captured his smile. "Oh hell no."

He said it so calmly, this is not okay. We all followed the eye line of Carder and looked at the house's front window.

My life has had many plot twists, some good, some obviously horrible. I have to say this plot twist I did NOT see this coming, nor did I want to even guess it would ever happen.

"They adopted a little boy. Like a fricken replacement!"

All of our eyes strained to see the three people moving about in the house. I can't even express how awful I feel, how awful Carder must feel inside.

"I'm all for adoption, and the kid is cute, probably ten or so, but what in the actual hell! I'm calling child services."

Lunging over the bags, I snatched the phone out of his hand. "Carder, this is some incredibly genuine bullshit, but we can't call child services."

"Yes, we can. Did you see the outfit they put him in? That's child abuse! Wait-" Pausing a moment, he looked back at the window and began to rapidly hit his seat. "That's my sweater! THEY KEPT MY SWEATER AND GAVE IT TO HIM; WHAT DID THEY NAME HIM CARDER GEORGE ELIZONDO TOO!?"

This just escalated to a whole new level. Thank God Jude intervened; for a moment, I felt like we were in the hands of a screenplay writer for a soap opera.

"Carder," Jude turned towards him and talked calmly but not patronizingly. "You literally have every right to be pissed off; I'm really sorry. The council is putting the commands of this mission in your control, but murder is off the table."

Carder didn't look at the house at all. "I would like to request a seat change with Lucy if that's okay, and we can get back on track. I'm sorry, guys."

He and I stepped out of the Jeep, but before Carder took his seat in the back, I gave him a big hug and whispered to him that there was nothing to be sorry about and that I was sorry too.

Then we were back on the road, and our adventure continued. Jude and I silently agreed it would be best to keep it quiet in the musical Jeep for a while; I had a feeling Carder was going to try and get a nap in.

And after about a half hour of silence, I was correct. Peering behind my seat was little Carder in the same position I was in before. Except he was lying on his stomach, which looked highly uncomfortable, but hey, whatever works.

I turned back around to my only awakened company. I felt some major Déjà vu; what could this remind me of? I've never driven outside of the city limits.

Wait.

Yepp.

It was registering now.

This reminded me of my first date with Jude.

Well, he wasn't Jude yet.

He was Sherlock.

And I still hadn't decided if that was declared an official date.

Granted, we did hold hands.

Briefly, I might add, *and* out of death looking us in the eye.

Never again will I go on that death trap of a ride.

"I feel so bad for him." Jude quietly spoke as I exchanged a look at Carder, and then back to him. "He deserves so much better; I can't imagine not having a supportive family."

Letting out a sigh, I responded. "Carder really does. I know, and I know he sometimes knows he comes off a bit rough, but honestly, I don't blame him. He's gotten the short end of the stick so many times; *I know life isn't fair*, but for a one-time exception, I wish his life could be."

I felt Jude looking at me and turning, I was correct. "I'm glad he has you and your family. Your parents seem to care for him a lot which is awesome." Jude gave me a small smile.

"My parents love him." A giggle fleeted from me as a memory triggered.

"The first time they met him was picking up the both of us from after-school detention; he didn't have a ride. We were in band together, and a game the class played when either our teacher wasn't in the room or their back was turned was tossing a drumstick across the room. We would see how many times we could toss it back and forth until they returned. While trying to beat the high score, I tossed the stick to Carder. As I released the drumstick and he caught it, the teacher turned around and immediately grew furious. We didn't rat the class out; we took the fall, but Carder wouldn't go without arguing back. When we both got in the car, my parents were upset obviously and asked what we did, and after explaining, they both couldn't stop laughing. That night Carder came over for dinner and became a part of our family." Just like I could hear my parent's passed laughter, Jude was laughing along with them.

"He and Colin clicked right away. Gosh, those two were a riot."

Jude's goony smile was on vacation for a while, but I'm glad it was back on the job. That specific smile has its own way of making me feel all giddy inside.

"Any stories about those two?" Jude asked as I took a breath in. "Oh, but you don't have to if you aren't really in the mood. I totally understand, I'm sorry, I really gotta plan out what I say in my head before I just go off about topics that could be potentially sensitive, goodness gracious-"

My inhale turned into an exhaled laugh. "Jude, Jude, Jude, stop." Smiling at him though his eyes were on the road. "I'm completely fine with telling you a story. In fact, I just thought of one. Okay, so Carder is a culinary master, and Colin can't bake at all; a Home Economics class was required at our school. It was Colin's sophomore year, and he had all A's except for that class. His final was to bake something and bring it in; Colin really wanted to get straight A's.

Carder was ecstatic to take on his project, he went on and on about how his cupcakes were going to be the best damn cupcakes Virginia has ever seen. They planned to meet at Carder's locker before Colin's class started. So, Carder was handing the pan of cupcakes over to Colin, and as he spun around to speed to class, the cupcakes went flying as he ran into no other than his Home Economics teacher. She was covered in frosting. Oh my gosh, I didn't let that go for months. It was too great."

In full laughter, that I couldn't help joining in, Jude turned to me for a second and then focused back on the road. "That right there is legendary, I wish it was on tape. I'm really craving some delicious cupcakes now."

"Oh great, now I want cake." I laughed and imagined a perfectly round cake with buttercream frosting and sprinkles. Lots of rainbow sprinkles.

"The great thing about a wedding is the cake, which I have been told there will be plenty of, to fill our dessert needs."

"Perfect! 'Cause, I gotta say, I'm running pretty low; this girl needs some cake."

In almost unison, but with a millisecond delay on my part, we caught each other's gaze. Taking the bits of the memory I had just shared floating about my mind, I imagined Jude's face covered in frosting, like someone threw cake at him. This shouldn't be that entertaining. And surprisingly enough- No, it wouldn't be that surprising to me. Jude would definitely be placed in a situation that involved cake being thrown at him. It's pretty realistic in a fun way. As I've come to learn, anything, surprises, and all can happen in the presence of Jude Keats Johnson.

"Miss Lucy?"

Hadn't heard that in a while. "Why yes, Sir Jude?" I kinda missed it too.

"Oh, I like that!" The little crack of interest in his voice was adorable. "I was wondering if you'd like to continue our game?"

Seizing any lingering thoughts, his question confused me a little. "Aaaaand what...game...would this be?" I ended it with a small laugh, but this tiny new mystery still was trekking in my mind.

Playfully one of his hands hit his chest in 'shock' as he gasped and returned his hand to the wheel. "Why–" Pauses make for a nice dramatic effect. "Our game from our first night on the Boardwalk, of course."

Whelp, case closed. My brain was steps behind the smile that spread across my face after realizing what Jude was referring to.

"How completely foolish of me!" Making him, and quietly myself, laugh with my extravagant hand motions. "I would very much enjoy continuing, but

I can't remember whose turn it is."

He thought about it for a second. "I actually can't recall either; I'll go unless you have one in mind?"

Gesturing to him, he did the honors.

"Okay, let's see," I was reflecting Jude's signature goofy smile in anticipation of his question. "What way do you hold hands?"

He carried on, breaking out into what looked like a slightly nervous but contained confidence.

"You know, some people like holding hands like this," With his pause, I looked at him and saw he wasn't looking at me, but his hand was extended my way. "Only if you'd like to; you absolutely don't have to. But I do promise, my hands are not sweaty." Making me laugh yet again, I nervously placed my hand over his as he gently intertwined his fingers between mine and held my hand.

Well, he didn't lie. His hand was not sweaty. It was actually a bit cold from the wind. I could feel the small heat transfer from my palm to his. My eyes were locked on this display, it was so simple and almost perfect in the situation and environment we were in.

Oh gosh, I hope my hand isn't sweaty. I wonder if Jude has ever held hands with someone, well other than his mom, maybe his dad, he has probably held hands with Julia, and of course, now me-

Abruptly I pulled my fingers out between his and cupped my hand around his instead. Yes, yes, this is better.

Jude took a peek and smiled as his eyes adjusted back to the road. "I like this way too."

In agreement, I smiled. As if Jude could hear my smile. I held his hand a few seconds longer until they slipped from each other, his hand returning to the wheel.

It was brief, "Alrighty, Miss Lucy, you're up!" but nice.

I'm horrible at this game, as I remember the last time we played.

I had a question that slipped right out of my mouth before my brain thought about the pros and cons of said inquiry.

I swear this brain has a mind of its own-

Oh, oh, Lucy, your mind is even embarrassed for you.

"When was the last time you did something for the last time?"

Seeing Jude's eyebrows rise just a tad, I was worried that this question had more cons than pros.

"Hmm, well, the only one that comes to mind right now is the last time I played on my piano in the loft of our now old family home. But I'm sure I'll find another special place to play, that was a clever question! I liked that!"

Thank God.

"Alright, let's see, a question for Lucy." His fingers tapped on the wheel in thought. "It has to be a good one. You're far wittier than I am."

My cheeks may have turned a very light shade of pink, but I gave him a nudge.

"It doesn't compare to yours, but here we go: how many kisses have you had in your life?"

Oh, ew, past kisses. "Oh gosh," I felt myself automatically readjust in my seat to buy some time before answering. Talking about past romances isn't my strong suit. "Well, there were only two, really. Seth, and a resident's Grandson from my previous job at the nursing home. He would come in and visit often, he was a year older than me. It wasn't anything too extravagant. We went out a few times, but he completely cut me off for some reason, and I never saw him again. But I got over it."

It got awkward really quick after my last word tumbled out. "Anyway!"

Success!

The awkwardness has been broken!

But now I needed to think of a question, fast.

I'm having a major blank.

What could I possibly ask?

Nothing interesting was coming to mind.

Well, there was *something*.

Reaching discreetly into my pocket as my fingertips were met "Jude" with the thin paper material that was in Carder's slashed tire, "Umm-"I wanted to pull it out and ask him what this could mean and why it was even there. "Do you still want to be a Train Conductor?"

But something in me retreated from my warm pocket where the peculiar evidence would stay, for now.

Again, his fingers danced along the steering wheel, tapping into the beat of what I would think to be the rhythm inside his thoughts, thinking up his answer. His fingers took a break.

"You know, I really don't know." One finger tapped. "I haven't really given it thought these days." Just a short-lived tap.

"No, no, no," Playfully shaking my head with each repeated word. "That's no answer, and you know it."

Letting out an exaggerated fake sigh, he continued. "Well, I don't know; it seems pretty far off."

"Wait, what?" Lifting my leg, I rested it on my seat as I turned my body towards him. "Far off?"

Jude shrugged his shoulders for an answer.

"Jude, if you want to be a Train Conductor, there's no doubt in my mind you can make that happen. It's just a matter of whether you want it or not-"

"If you *need* an answer, then it's no, okay? It's not a priority."

I was shocked, in that moment, I hadn't seen his eyes change from the bright cheerfulness they are usually filled with to, a soft glaze I couldn't make out.

Anger?

Irritation?

I didn't think I was being pushy, or too forward, but I also didn't think he'd give up that dream.

I do know that it was something I wouldn't bring up again.

With that, I moved back, facing forward as this silent notion from our council of two passed an agreement of quiet time and an end to our game.

The next few hours consisted of a variety of old tunes. Vague but polite requests for a new cassette to be pushed in, a few times, we both caught ourselves singing a chorus, and on one stop when Carder woke up, we traded spots.

Just a few more hours until we would finally arrive in New York. Oh my gosh, that's insane. The music kept flowing through as I returned to my lying-down position.

I don't think Jude is mad at me. Of course, I've never seen him angry, so I have nothing to compare it to.

If he was angry, though, I don't think he'll hold it for that long; maybe I could apologize.

Apologize for what exactly, though; *Sorry, I brought up something that is apparently sensitive.*

Wow, that was a bit much.

Perhaps Jude is mad at me.

But I also overthink.

Contemplating all these emotions and thoughts, my unused ones decided it was time for a break. Time to drift off; I could feel I had already begun to slip away into nap world quite a few conscionable questions ago.

Down down I went,

Cascade from each and every argument.

Down down I go,

Ditch reality far below.

"Lucy!" I felt a hand on my shoulder, quickly shaking me. "Lucy-Lou, wake up!"

Lucy-Lou? Only Carder calls me that. Opening my eyes, I saw it was Carder, his body turned to the back seat, his hand still on my shoulder. And Jude was there; why was I dreaming of this?

"Look! We're here! We are actually HERE! LUCY!" Carder was ecstatic as Jude laughed with his excitement.

At least he's in a better mood.

Wait–

I looked out and saw a beauty you couldn't find in Virginia Beach: New York City.

"Carder, was I sleeping?"

"Yea, as soon as your head hit the seat, you were out, I wanted to let you sleep, but I wanted you to see this more!" He was glowing, radiating this pure delight that shined brighter than the sun in my eyes.

So, I actually woke up.

I wasn't dreaming of any of this.

This was happening.

THIS WAS HAPPENING.

I'm, we're, in New York City.

But I didn't dream of anything; it didn't even feel like I had slept at all.

There were so many buildings. They didn't look much different than the ones in Virginia Beach. Not at all, but they felt different to be around.

The little musical Jeep was now traveling with a sea of cars, cabs, buses, mopeds, and even bikes! Passengers in each of them, with their own adventures in mind.

You could feel the adrenaline of potential and exhilaration souring through the wind between the hums of musicians, weaving through the different sounds and conversations people were having, and all of it belonged to everyone.

This feeling couldn't be bought; it was shared.

Being brought up to speed, Julia texted Jude the new family home address, and we followed the GPS's blunt directions. According to the all-so-intelligent and sassy machine, we were to arrive in about forty minutes

3. The Grand Johnson Estate 

"No," Exchanging a look at Carder, who was bouncing in his seat. "You're joking."

I was nervous about letting my eyes drift to the rearview mirror, where I knew I would be met with Jude's. Alas, when they finally focused, his eyes were waiting for me.

But he didn't look upset in the slightest. He seemed very amused with the unbelievable excitement overflowing the Jeep.

I guess he's not one to hold onto something; I'm glad it blew over. There's a tiny bit of discomfort floating about my gut from not confronting it; right now wasn't the time, though now was the time to flip out.

"Believe it or not," Jude began to speak in a cheerful tone. "I'm just as surprised as you guys are, I have to say I think my parents have overdone it."

Overdone it was an understatement. Maybe even a false statement. I could not wrap my mind around this.

THIS is HIS house?

This lucky son of a gun.

Jude typed some keypad password on the gate Julia had sent him via text so we could get in; once we did, the Jeep made its way on the long driveway to the house.

It was breathtaking, literally, though; Carder smacked my leg after realizing I was holding my breath unconsciously.

The driveway path stretched down to the house and had a rounded curve you would drive down to head out. Between these paths was a lovely-looking pound with small trees and flowers.

The house–the word *house* is an insult to this *mansion*.

That doesn't seem to do justice, either.

This was a mansion on steroids.

We'll put it this way, Jude's new family home is HUGE.

The whole property was surrounded by willow, oak, and birch trees. I've never seen so many beautiful trees; I hope they tipped their landscaper- big time.

Approaching closer, I could see now that there were three separate structures. There was the huge main one we blatantly noticed straight ahead. Then to the side, off a small path from the driveway, there were two adorable buildings. They had a cottage feel to them as they were tucked away within the collage of trees.

As Jude parked the Jeep, we heard a door slam; turning in reaction, we saw an ecstatic and sprinting Julia, almost tackling her brother down. While this was happening, some quite loud shrieks of excitement came from her until she reached him. Oh gosh, this is just too cute.

"My baby brother! Ah! How I've missed you!" She squeezed him in a hug between each exclamation and kissed his cheeks with sisterly love. "I'm so glad you're here; we have so much to do."

Her gaze shifted as we received the same embrace but no kisses. I can't say I'm complaining about that. Just as Julia released us, Jude began to talk.

"It's great to see you too, sis. Is anyone else home right now?"

Looking at Julia, she shook her head. "Nah, not right now. Dad is with Angelo at the airport to help him pick up his family. They aren't *all* flying in, sad enough, but quite a few of them were able to make it, which is great! Angelo's family means so much to him; he misses them an awful lot. Oh!" Giving Jude a small punch on the arm. "Angelo got a kick out of my Maid of Honor announcement; he can't wait to see you!"

She giggled with this little smirk as Jude's cheeks began to faintly turn a soft shade of pink while Julia started to explain.

"Well, you see, I've never really had a girl best friend, and Jude has been my best friend forever, so it was only fitting to make him my maid of honor."

"And no, I will not be wearing a dress," Jude stated like he could read Carder's thoughts.

I just know for a fact that Carder is mentally picking him out a dress. Work it, Jude.

Julia threw her arm over his shoulders. "Sad enough, we couldn't convince him."

They both gave each other a playful nudge while Carder was already losing it, using me as a crutch, which wasn't working too well because I was laughing just as much.

"Okay, okay, but we gotta get down to business, its tomor- Oh my gosh. Jude. Jude, it's *tomorrow*." Julia tried to catch her breath to her realization.

Jude put his hands on her shoulders, counseling her to breathe and reassuring her everything would get done. He then offered Julia his arm to escort her to the main house; they both turned to Carder and me, displaying that lovely Johnson smile.

"Sorry for the meltdown, guys; it keeps hitting me. This is actually happening!"

"Goodness, no, no need to apologize." Carder kindly replied as I nodded in agreement.

"Yes, we completely understand. Is there anything Carder and I can do to help?"

Without looking at Jude, Julia answered. "Heavens, no, you two are my-" Now she quickly glanced at Jude before turning back to us. "Our guests. And if I could be a bit bold, I'd love to have some brother-sister time before the big day. It's nothing at all against you; I'm really looking forward to hanging out later tonight! Us four and some of Angelo's cousins, it'll be legendary!"

Oh boy, that's a riot to look forward to.

"I've actually arranged something for the both of you anyway after hearing it's your first time in NYC."

Jude's eyebrows raised as his eyes floated from mine to Julia's; her confident smile overcame the temporary mood of confusion.

"In about thirty minutes, a car will pull up. It's one of my dad's best drivers. He will take you anywhere in the city you'd like. I can't take all the credit, though; dad was happy to provide his services. But until then, make yourselves at home. The guest house is that one on the right." Like New York's best tour guide, Julia pointed out as Carder and I looked in confirmation.

"You can check out the place and claim your room. If you don't mind, I must steal my Maid of Honor for a while." Julia gave us a wink while pulling Jude along by her side, now going into the main house.

Before the door closed, Jude looked over his shoulder and gave us a pretend 'panic' face. Carder and I just gave him a sassy wave and laughed as he gave us a 'glare' while shutting the door.

Before either of us spoke up, we took in our surroundings, completely awestruck, until I felt a grip on my forearm. The hold of what one would guess, a giddy teenager in the presents of their favorite boy band. But we all know that grip belongs to beloved Carder.

"Can you believe this? Lucy, look around! Look at this luxurious shit; it's overwhelming with greatness!" Once he realized his hand wrapped tighter with each word, like a blood pressure cuff, he apologetically released my arm.

"Sorry, I'm sorry, I'm just so excited; this is crazy!"

I couldn't be upset with the goofy smile on Carder's face that matched the glimmer in his eyes. I love seeing him so excited.

Clearing his throat as if he couldn't get sillier, he spoke with an impressively executed British accent, "Shall we take a stroll around the manor, madam?"

Giggling with a nod, we started our walk; when I tried to speak, my vocal cords also tightened from excitement. With a few deep breaths, my throat finally loosened up, and I couldn't agree with Carder more. It all was beautiful, completely and utterly flawless.

It was like I walked into the fricken Secret Garden with the path I stumbled upon. While walking, I could see where Carder and I would stay for the weekend.

Like I was in my own fantasy land, I imagined that's where we actually lived. I was just out for a morning stroll before going inside to heat up some water for my french press coffee. My favorite mug, purchased for 75 cents at an antique store tucked away in Manhattan, and a deeply adored book waiting on a cute little table for two inside.

Ah, what a dream.

All these trees had me thinking about me and Colin's tree-climbing obsession growing up. Lord knows why, but I know if we had grown up here, our parents would have never seen us during the day unless they climbed up one themselves. The thought of Mom climbing a tree, I shouldn't laugh, but it's just too great of a visual.

I almost felt a hint of guilt, a secret betrayal that I was stepping on this grass.

This grass is prettier than me.

While watching my feet lightly step on the lawn, I found myself in front of our little home for the weekend. Smiling, I turned to ask Carder if- If Carder was by me, I could have asked him. Turning the other way, I didn't see him anywhere. I swear, we're in New York for less than an hour, and he's already lost-

Vibrate

Vibrate

Vibrate

Of course, it's him. "Carder, where are you?" Answering the phone like an angry mother.

"Lucy."

Oh my gosh, can we have one conversation that isn't dramatically built up? "Carder."

"Lucy, don't get mad, but I have no idea where I am."

I had to take the phone away from my ear as I heard him repeat my name until I brought the phone back up. "How?"

"Luc-"

"How?! How could you get lost?!" I was trying not to angry laugh.

"I don't know! I thought you were following me, and we were quiet."

"Carder."

"You know, like embracing the moment, best friend and best friend."

"Carder."

"And then I look, and you aren't there, and I started jumping to conclusions,"

"Carder"

"It would be so easy to abduct you,"

"Carder!"

"What?!"

Really? What? Is that what he has to say, "What are you by?"

"Umm, one sec," Hearing Carder lower his phone as he was probably looking around. "I'm close to the pier, so I'm walking to it right now."

Pier? What in the hell- "Where's the pier?"

"In the back of the big big big house!"

Internally I laughed because I could see the house diagram in his mind: The main house was the big big big house. The one guest house was the big big house. And the guest house we were staying in was the big house. Oh, Carder, sweet, sweet Carder.

"See you in a few!" Hearing the click before I even got a word in. Not that it would have made a difference, but whatever.

Taking another glance at the big house, I turned my back and began to make my way to this pier Carder speaks of. We'd better keep track of the time to catch that ride into the city.

Wow, that sounded super cool, like a high-budget secret agent movie.

I don't think I'd make it long in one of those movies, and Carder would definitely get shot for being sassy.

Making my way to the back of the big big big house, the yard was enormous, almost to the point of being a bit overwhelmed by the fountain and garden that was in front of me. Past its beauty, I could see the pier. And a figure with its back faced me, admiring the water and city afar. I could see now how Carder might have managed to get lost. I felt misplaced in my own thoughts looking at the landscape. My feet seemed to be the only ones on task, as I hadn't noticed I was already walking through the large-flowered garden. I'd be steps away from the pier in a few moments.

"Carder!" Calling out as he turned in reaction with a smile on his face. Waving me over, I hustled to where he was, gently running into him on purpose for wandering off on me. "Well, hello again, stranger," Giving him a playful wink and a nudge while, in return, he gave a roll of his eyes and then a goofy smile.

Which, of course, made my smile turn all goony and whatnot,

Damnit, Carder.

"I'm sure that car will be here soon. Shall we get going?" I gestured to him, starting to walk with a hop of excitement in my step, but noticing he hadn't moved; he hadn't moved at all. Slightly I tilted my head in confusion as I poked his shoulder. "Everything alright there?"

I could tell he was zoning out.

Not even a minute before, he seemed perfectly fine,

Maybe even happier than I was with just the simple fact he was on this pier.

But now, his eyes were fixed on the skyline of the city.

Curious,

I settled my eyes on the sight as well;

I knew without looking that it was beautiful,

Sometimes we assume beauty, I guess.

But I was puzzled why he seemed so sucked into it now at this moment.

"Sorry!" Jolting out of his trance, laughing it off, "It was just sinking in, you know? I mean, in Virginia Beach, we have buildings like that, but we don't have buildings like that."

That was precisely what I was thinking, but I didn't have the words for it. It's kind of funny how a different arrangement of tall buildings makes an entirely different world.

Here I felt anxious but terribly excited to the point where my hands felt jittery, like I couldn't handle the adrenaline, but I craved more.

A sense of determination, though in all honesty, I had no idea what we would do in the Big Apple.

So, I suppose you could say I was also feeling a bit spontaneous.

But I also felt,

Lost.

But not lost like before when I felt lost in my thoughts,

Or right now, I guess, as I'm dancing around in them.

No,

I felt lost without-

"Yea," Carder gently touched my arm. "Let's make our way to the front, onwards to our grand adventure Lucy-Lou!"

Colin.

We raced there, like kids sprinting through their Mother's garden though they've been told several times not to, and they feel more of a rush than guilt as their laughter ignitions their imagination.

Oh, what these trees could be if I was still seven years old.

We got there just in the nick of time; our breath caught up to us as Mr. Johnson's apparent best driver pulled up to the house.

I'm guessing Jude heard the car as he came out of the house to send us off on our first-ever New York City voyage.

"Oh my gosh, I'm so excited for both of you!" Softly touching my shoulder as he went past Carder and me to open the backseat door. "And finally, to introduce you to one of the coolest guys I know, sir Aden Alvarez!" Approaching the car, hunching over just enough to get a good look at this famous driver and,

Wow.

He's not what I pictured for a New York driver.

In movies, they always have some cranky old guy who looks like he cut himself shaving and is in desperate need of a cigarette break, but this,

this Aden Alvarez guy,

well, he was,

not hard to look at, that's for sure.

Giving us a friendly smile, shifting his eyes to each of us, so we all felt welcomed in his nice black car, Jude continued the introduction.

"I'm sorry I can't stick around longer and accompany you guys. Julia needs someone to not only help her out but also help keep her sanity in check. At least until after the wedding ceremony; then the nerve-wracking stuff is over, and we can party it up!" We all chuckled while he gave Aden a knuckle touch, and me and Carder a wave goodbye.

4. NYC, Party of Two 

Iscooted in first; Carder shut the door softly because this was one hell of a nice car. It was shiny like some little elf came in every morning and scrubbed each inch with his magical shining polish.

The silence was brewing as we began to make our way out of the gated neighborhood. Not an entirely awkward silence, but there was a vibe of obligation to speak up after the introduction.

But who would be up for such a task?

Why I think we all know who it is.

"Your car is very clean."

Wrong!

It was me,

Point for Lucy.

Alas, I was not successful. If anything, it shifted to total awkward silence now.

I'm not taking my point away, though.

I tried.

Carder turned to me and mouthed back what I said in the form of a question, like *'why on Earth would I utter those words out loud.'*

Throwing him an insulted expression, we both turned forward as we heard the sound of our driver nonchalantly clearing his throat.

"Well, thank you, that's very kind of you to say." We made eye contact for a second through the review mirror.

Remarkable how much impact that split moment had on releasing buckets full of butterflies in my stomach. Aden had this soft voice, but it wasn't straining to hear. It was like, if Poetry was a person, this would be him.

"So where shall we go? I'll take you anywhere in the city you'd like!"

Again he smiled at me through the rearview mirror, or maybe he was smiling at both me and Carder. I don't know; I overanalyze everything.

Truthfully, I don't have much knowledge of New York besides all the basics I learned throughout school. As far as entertainment goes, I have no clue.

I need to be cultured.

"Carder, any ideas?" I asked in a hopeful tone.

He pondered for a second until he turned his attention from the view passing us through the window to me. "I'll do whatever you'd like." Giving me a smile, I didn't want to return because I hated being in the position to decide. But come on, I had to give him one back; it was too cheery of a smile to ignore.

I didn't think Aden heard the sigh I released, but embarrassingly enough, I was wrong. "Might I suggest something?"

"Yes please!" Aden laughed at my enthusiasm while I felt the playful judgment radiating off Carder.

"I would suggest Coney Island; it's fun and full of adventure." He turned his head back to us both for a moment to give us the full view of that captivating gaze.

Which captivated me to the point of my audio plug-in malfunctioning momentarily. I didn't even hear what he had said. "I'm sorry, what was that?"

Although he laughed, I still felt a tad bit dumb. "It's no problem; I said you two look like adventurers, so it may be the perfect place! But like I said before, I will take you wherever you'd like."

Naturally, Carder and I agreed with Aden on his suggestion.

I know my reasoning.

I wouldn't be surprised if Carder was on the same mesmerized page.

Or if he just agreed because I did.

Regardless it doesn't really matter.

Up next,

Carder,

Lucy,

and their journey to Coney Island!

It looked super busy when we arrived; Aden informed us it's always this way when the weather is nice. A crowd is nothing Carder and I couldn't handle, though.

We agreed that Carder and I would call Aden when we wanted to be picked up and go on our next adventure. This was a win-win because I guess

Aden had errands to run anywho.

And now Carder and I can say we got the phone number of a cute guy in NYC! I don't know who we would brag about this with. I guess our only real option is Alan. That could be amusing.

There was so much color,

Culture,

People,

Yea, there were a TON of people.

But my favorite thing about this place is that it was like a little piece of home I brought with me.

The lights, carnival games, the beach, rides, and so many different lives are off in a scurry and carelessly interrupting others. Almost everywhere I looked, I could see a little piece of Virginia Beach.

I suppose if you look hard enough wherever you end up, though, you could find something, some kind of connection to the place you left behind.

Thankfully putting a stop to my thoughts before I get carried away, Carder put my hand around his arm.

"First order of business; we are not getting lost for a second time today." With a playful tap on my hand, he continued, "Second, what shall we do first?! I mean, this place is no V.B. Boardwalk, but I must say, it's pretty dandy, don't ya think?"

He was acting like a '50s Carder. That's actually a fun thought, a version of Carder placed in the '50s.

His hair combed neatly to the side, not a strand out of place,

A cute sweater vest over his white dress shirt and tie,

Some nice slacks.

Yes.

I said Slacks.

And shiny dress shoes.

If we were living in this time, I wouldn't mind rocking some high-waist shorts and skirts; but I'd prefer my independence now.

Now is good.

"Oh my gosh," I felt Carder's arm tense and then relax again. "Lucy, I feel like *Audrey Hepburn.*"

Pulling back from him, "What?" But still having my hand wrapped around his arm, "No! No, I'm *Audrey,*"

"Hell no, you're not taking Audrey; you be some other cliché New Yorker."

I gave him a fake pout and a few stomps of my feet. We got some looks, which I was aiming for, and Carder hates that.

Public ridicule for the win.

"You can be *Annie.*"

Oh, "The *orphan,* Annie, *that Annie,*" Now he's done it.

"Yes, Lucy, it's a classic."

"I'm not an orphan!"

"Have you ever cared to explore your options?"

"I don't even have curly hair!"

"What, you have something against adorable, hardworking orphans now? Is that it?"

Okay, that made me chuckle a little "Carder-"

"Lucy! You Monster!"

"Oh my gosh, shut up," Letting out a full laugh as we continued to argue about who could be who.

If he got to be Audrey, I would break the gender roles and be Jack Kelly from the Newsies.

And with that, we both envisioned and agreed I could most certainly rock suspenders.

We chatted about an off-Broadway show where *Newsies* meets *Breakfast at Tiffany's* until we saw the possibility of our first Coney Island experience. We didn't even ask one another if we wanted to go on it. We both just walked right into the line and awaited our turn.

Our turn on *The Wonder Wheel*, Coney Islands' famous Ferris Wheel.

When we stepped on the small platform leading up to our wobbly seat where a tween couple had just got off, giggling away,

Blah,

Isn't it sickening?

Oh, I'm just joshing,

They were actually pretty cute.

Go on, you crazy-mindless-in love- kids!

Anyway, as we got on and had the bar secured across our laps, the wheel began to spin, along with my eyes looking at this fantastic view. I could just vaguely hear the bits of conversations of the other passengers.

The couple in front of us was hilarious.

Before getting on the ride, it's clearly written out to not rock the seats,

but of course, some people just can't help themselves when it comes to experiencing certain danger in a public setting.

The couple consisted of this tall and a bit lanky-looking guy and a gal with a bit of a wild side. The girl kept rocking the seat, laughing her head off, while the guy screamed bloody murder each time their seat swung.

Chanting out some ridiculous saying each time, like-

Well, now he just shouted some odd combination of-

Chemistry terms?

Actually, I didn't know what he was shouting until Carder mumbled the question, '*Why in the hell is this guy screaming out Chemistry nonsense in place of swear words?*' under his breath to me.

Regardless, it didn't stop being funny even after our second loop around; man, this guy must really love her.

I wasn't sure how many times the ride went around until our turn was over. As I was about to ask Carder if he had a wild guess, we reached the very top of the Ferries Wheel, and our ride abruptly stopped.

Causing our fellow rider in front of us to scream formulas once again.

And Carder, startled as I, grabbed my arm in reaction to the unexpected halt.

We both looked at each other, puzzled, of course, then Carder cautiously looked over our seat down below to see what had happened.

"See anything?" Asking him, trying not to let the panic taint the calm tone I had going on.

Way to go, survival-skills-Lucy.

"I have no idea. The ride attendant isn't even at his post thingy." Carder leaned out a little more, scaring the crap out of me as I eased him back. "And I'm going to assume you can hear that screaming from down there, so I don't need to explain that."

"What?!" My first reaction was to lean over him and look for myself. I had heard screaming, but we were in a carnival setting. There was noise coming from everywhere. I refrained from looking over Carder and remained seated. "What in the hell is going on down there?!"

Carder was surprisingly calm. "I have no clue. I don't see him or any employees for that matter down there,"

Or he was irritated on another level that doesn't deserve his energy and sassiness. "Mr. Coney is going to get a piece of my mind." Ah, nope, there it is.

Audrey, your Carder is showing.

Slouching without making any vast movement of our seat, I let out a sigh to follow up his remark, "Yea, this is just spectacular."

"What in the literal hell, though, who does this?! Fricken Sociopaths doing an experiment on how long humans can last in fear at 150 ft in the air?"

I was going to make a *Sherlock* reference, it was tough not to, but Carder most likely would have thrown me out of our seat if I did.

"And don't you dare make a damn *Sherlock* reference."

Called it. "Alright, let's not get like the guy in front of us," I managed in a whisper. "I'm sure everything is fine."

Just as Carder, I'm guessing, was going to make some smartass remark, my phone started ringing.

Pulling it out to reveal a Facetime call from Mr. Jude himself.

Extending my arm out to fit the both of us in the camera's frame, I answered.

As Jude came into focus, I could see he was sitting at a kitchen counter. A very fancy one, too, I may add.

I'm sure everything there is on good terms with the adjective fancy.

"Guys! Hey! How's NYC?!" Excitingly he asked. While his words were coming to a stop, a confused expression punched in while his giddy smile took a lunch break. "Sorry, where exactly are you guys?"

This time I tried to speak before Carder to explain; keyword tried.

"We are currently stuck at the fricken top of this fricken Ferris Wheel at Coney fricken Island." At least it was straightforward, I suppose. "The ride just stopped out of nowhere a few minutes ago. We've just been sitting here."

Nodding in agreement, Jude looked more terrified than I'd imagine Carder and I combined looked.

"Oh my gosh, oh my gosh, you guys hang tight; I'm so sorry this happened; oh my gosh, okay, calm, I'm going to hang up. Find the number to the help desk or something at Coney Island, and see what's going on, don't panic, guys; it'll be okay!"

Carder did not take that suggestion to heart. "Don't tell me not to panic! You're panicking! I'm not panicking! No one is panicking over here except Professor Awkward in front of us!"

Goodness gracious, Carder, would you like some humanity with that unmerciful lashing? I gave him a hit on the leg, which wasn't visible to Jude.

"Okay, I'll try not to either," Jude hasn't even known Carder long, and he knows it's better not to argue with him about these sorts of things. "I'll call you back ASAP!" They grow up so fast.

After he hung up and pocketed the phone, I shifted my body towards Carder. "Hey, what was that all about?"

Not looking at me at first, he turned his body like I did with mine and acted utterly oblivious. "What is what all about?"

"Okay, don't even start that. You know you were acting super rude to Jude."

I hate when I accidentally rhyme at serious moments like this. The poet within me chimes in at the worst times. "You're just acting strange, is all."

I might as well have asked Carder to pretend we were in some low-budget soap opera after spilling that line.

He gave me a very fake sarcastic laugh. "Well, I'm SoooOOooRRRrrYyyyY. I may be a bit cranky being stuck in a dumpster seat at literally the highest point of this ride."

Rolling my eyes, which I don't think he saw, I turned to look out my side of our 'dumpster seat.'

He'll cool off; we'll be okay, I'm sure.

I have this doubt that his outburst is regarding the ride being stuck, but then again, I have been wrong many times before.

And we may be stuck, but at least we were stuck in some sort of paradise.

I kept thinking about all the people down there, the people I was watching from up here.

I wonder if any of them looked up at the Ferris Wheel and noticed it had stopped or even looked and saw the little specks at the very top and wondered how they must be feeling right now.

I wonder if any of them have been to Virginia Beach,

Or even lived there at one point in their lives.

I thought about 'Professor Awkward' and his riot of a gal and wondered how long they had been together.

How did they meet?

Was this their first date?

I know how those Boardwalk-let's go on this ride-that seems like a good idea- first dates are.

Wait, still have not decided if that was a date.

Maybe I should just say it is; what else would it be?

Damnit, this is confusing.

That about sums up life.

Vibrate

Vibrate

Vibrate

How does he do that?

I answered Jude's phone call with the tiniest bit of hope. "Hey, any good news?" My voice turned out a little more monotone than I would have liked, which I didn't mean; I was still puzzled about Carder's attitude.

"Yes!" Jude optimistically replied in his Judeness way.

"Great!" And now, in an attempt to redeem myself from sounding unexcited when I answered, I sounded like a 12-year-old going through puberty's first stages with the crack my voice made.

Which made Jude giggle a bit, and I couldn't blame him.

"Wait, let me put you on speaker."

After a second, Jude cleared his throat to deliver the news.

"Okay, so! It turns out the guy running the Ferris Wheel is a big-time scratch ticket buyer like it's an addiction. His boss said he was going around all morning saying how he had the winning ticket. His boss was like, 'Frank, shut your lying ass up and get to work,' and Frank was like, 'If I win, I'm leaving this place!' and his boss was like, 'Frank, shut the hell up' and it turns out Frank indeed won, and he just left."

"So, Frank abandoned us?" I confirmed.

"Frank is an asshole," Carder also confirmed.

"Yes, Frank should have at least let everyone off the ride after he scratched his winning ticket. But you guys should be getting down any minute now because his boss sent someone over to the ride. I'm really sorry again. Do you want me to call Aden for you guys?"

I looked to Carder for an answer, and he gave me this gentle nod.

What is going on with him?

"Um, yea, yes, please, that'd be great." I was still looking at Carder, who was looking at the view and occasionally his feet. "Thank you, Jude, we appreciate it!"

"Yea, of course! It's my job as a New Yorker to ensure you have an awesome first time here. I'm sorry that happened, but fear not, I'm most positive the rest of your stay will be pleasant!"

Laughing at Jude's enthusiasm, he told me he would inform Aden about picking us up. From there, we could go anywhere in the city we wanted. And when we arrived back at the house, we would have a chillaxing time.

With another smile through the phone and a thank you, we said our goodbyes and ended the call.

Around twenty-ish minutes later, Aden picked us up in the super sleek spy car.

We climbed into the backseat, admired the city in comfortable silence, and explained our misfortunes with the Ferris Wheel.

But all the while, I couldn't stop wondering what was going on with Carder for the life of me.

He was acting so unusual.

We're in New York City!

He should be freaking out right now!

Taking a million pictures!

Having backseat driver road rage!

Anything besides what he's doing now.

Acting like a timid young man who only talks to his collectible model trains.

You know what,

That was rude,

I'm sure model trains are great company.

Besides the point, though;

Something was wrong, and at this point, I could tell he wasn't going to give in and admit something was wrong.

And when Aden asked where we'd like to stop next, and Carder replied that he'd like to go back to the house if that was alright with the two of us, that to me was his white flag.

5. A Map Is A Map 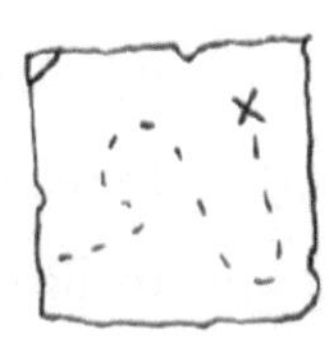

After Aden dropped us off at the Johnson's residence, he had to take off right away to finish the errands we interrupted him on with our malfunctioning Ferris Wheel experience.

I honestly didn't know what or, better yet, how even to approach Carder or confront this sudden mood change of his.

I cared about him, obviously, very much; we've been through a lot together. But this is a bit ridiculous. We traveled all this way to have the time of our lives, and it wasn't exactly easy to leave. This was supposed to be our big adventure! I just don't understand what was going on in his mind.

Jude opened the door for us, and as we approached the big big big house's front door, I wasn't surprised by the confused expression Jude had. And once again, it didn't come as a surprise when the expression reappeared when Carder asked him if it was alright to use the shower in the guest house and take a nap. Of course, Jude said yes. I don't think he would say no, even if Carder was a homeless guy shy of a few teeth.

Carder was off on his solitary mission without a simple wave goodbye or an explanation. At the same time, Mr. Johnson and I were left in puzzlement.

Surprise Surprise.

"Is everything okay?" Jude spoke up after a few moments of silence mixed with that feeling of obligation to say something.

"It'll be okay; maybe he's just tired or something."

Oh, wait, "No, actually," Now I feel like an idiot and the world's worst friend. "Maybe it's starting to really hit him. With everything that happened with his parents." After the realization escaped my lips, we both had an *'ah-ha'* moment.

We can share the world's worst friend award: I'll take the gold, and Jude will get the silver.

"Gosh, yea, that probably is it. I feel like an ass; why did that not cross my mind?"

"You have a lot on your mind, with the wedding and all. I should have known."

"Hey," Giving me a nudge with a simple but warming smile, "Don't beat yourself up about it. I think Carder just may need some time alone, you know? Get the crying, yelling, or maybe even singing out of his system so he can move on." Jude looked taken aback for a moment and then snapped back into our realization conversation. "Wow, that sounded harsher out loud than it did in my head."

I giggled, immediately feeling horrible after doing so. "It's just funny you say singing; Carder sings the big showstopper show tunes in the shower when he's had a rough day. One time, I heard him slip in the shower while belting out a note; it was priceless."

Laughing about a fond memory, I didn't feel so bad about it because I knew Carder would have laughed. But I couldn't help but think I could have prevented this situation if I had just asked Carder if he wanted to talk about it.

Jude's right, though; he needs some time to breathe.

My arm got another gentle nudge, looking at Jude, who had this grin on his face. A kind of grin that has some sort of plan behind it. A grin like that didn't come without some kind of mischief.

"I'm off the hook for a while; Julia ran off somewhere. Something about a flower crisis that I'm not allowed to venture with because I had laughed at said *'flower crisis'* codename. So, I'm not sure if she went alone or she's meeting my Mom there."

I wondered where that charming, rambling trait of his had gone off to,

"Anyway,"

It's been too long!

"I have something I want to show you. I actually haven't seen it in forever, so it's almost like a surprise for the both of us!" That little glisten in his eyes sealed the deal for me.

Nodding while beginning to follow his lead, he started to explain this surprise of ours.

"So, as we both know, I was at my place in lovely Virginia Beach when my folks moved here. With that, I couldn't pick my own room and decorate it and whatnot. Which I'm not upset about. Don't get me wrong; it's sweet and thoughtful that my parents want us to always have a place to go and call home."

Snickering under my breath at the adorable rambling, not very well apparently, he went on.

"Well, my Mom told me where my room is in the house, but that's it, so I'm not sure what to expect. I do, however, know of one item in the room. An item I dearly miss so much, I dare say, I may even miss it more than I miss pistachios." Jude turned his head to me for a moment, "I've been low on my daily pistachio intake for a few hours now; I don't know how I'm still standing."

After he was satisfied with my reaction to his dramatic joke, he adjusted his head forward again. "But for real though, I am so psyched! I may cry, so be emotionally and physically prepared, maybe even mentally, just to be safe. I'm an ugly crier."

As I was about to playfully push him for that last remark, I saw him pull a small, square piece of paper from his pocket. He brought it up close to his face, examining it carefully, which made my curiosity skyrocket. I went with the soft–clearing–the–throat attention-getter, and the outcome was perfect.

Jude gently turned and realized I was a little out of the loop.

"Oh heavens," This guy and his vocabulary, I tell ya, you never know what to expect.

"I could have sworn I was talking out loud; my apologies! So, when I said my Mom told me where my room was, I meant, well, yes, technically, she did, but not straightforward. That'd be much too easy; Mom doesn't do easy. Even when I'm not being homeschooled, she wants to stimulate the mind. Oh, but yes, this is her *telling me*- it's a map. A small and simple map, but a map is a map!"

How inspirational for maps everywhere.

"First here" He walked closer to me, bending his arm down so I could see this small map. "We have successfully made it down this hallway" Pointing out the short parallel lines, what a lovely drawn hallway. "And noowww,"

Dragging out his words as his finger slid with his verbal direction, "We shall turn right and walk across the middle room."

My eyebrows looked at each other in interest, "Middle room?"

Jude gave his explanation with a shrug. "Oh, I have no idea what to call this room, so I just call it the middle room."

As we walked to the edge of the said middle room, it made sense, a little.

It was this giant open space; along the sides were columns stretched to the ceiling, and a large skylight looked up to the top. The natural light that was gracing the room was absolutely stunning. Neither of us had crossed the room's threshold yet; we were mesmerized by its existence.

"Alright," I spoke out loud, the both of us still looking off into this bright open space. "This room is way too beautiful not to have its own name."

"You're right. Absolutely right."

"It just isn't okay."

"It's inhuman."

"Hmmm, inhuman,"

"It's inarchitectural?" Jude's eyes peeked at me before returning their attention to the unnamed room.

I nodded in approval. "Clever."

"Why, thank you."

"But still, where's the justice."

He paused before exclaiming excitingly, "How about" Putting out his hands, encouraging me to *envision* this new upcoming name, "*The Illuminating*

Ballroom?"

My thoughts caught up to the corners of my lips that curled up after the name was released. "Oh, so this is a ballroom, is it?"

Turning to see his lips were thinking the same as mine, "I'd say there is more than enough space to dance in here, wouldn't you say?"

Dance. The word triggered; brought me back to my heart-to-heart with Julia. When Jude was in the hospital, but he wasn't Jude yet, he was Sherlock. After the bee incident. According to her, he's never danced.

"Well," I had to find out for myself, "Shall we test that hypothesis?" I felt hopeful about this leap of courage. The atmosphere was perfect, and no music was needed for this experiment.

But as my eyes reached his, what sounded like a nervous laugh escaped him; his eyes were not so good at covering up the anxiousness that rose in him from my question.

"Wouldn't I love to, but alas, we mustn't get sidetracked from the mission!"

Experiment Outcome: Utter-Awkwardness-Failure.

"Yea, yea, of course!" Laughing it off, "I approve of the name, though."

"I am glad to hear it, Miss Lucy" The beaming kindness of his smile made the sting go away, as always.

So, the mission continued, as did the mystery that is Jude Johnson.

After crossing The Illuminating Ballroom's grand opening and feeling the sun's warmth on my skin, we made a left, and down another hallway, we went.

I could imagine his parents and Julia, perhaps Angelo as well, decorating this hallway; it certainly couldn't be done by one person.

Well, no I take that back. I'm sure one person could. It would just be one hell of a job.

Both walls of the hallway were covered in picture frames. I kid you not; the wallpaper underneath was hardly visible. As we walked down, I admired the pictures we passed, just little glimpses.

There was a picture of little Jude and little Julia by the Eiffel Tower, and

Julia and their Mom walking hand and hand in a pretty sunlit meadow.

Then we passed a picture of three children, all in short-sleeved shirts and shorts, sitting on a fallen tree; they must have been hiking or something outdoorsy. I could make out which was Jude and Julia, and that left their older brother Finley.

Tracking back to Julia's story, I remembered the painful story.

Their talented older brother.

Jude's secretive tattoo.

This is *Finley*.

Turning to Jude, I wanted to smile at him. These memories and captured moments aren't mine, but I wanted to reminisce with him.

But we reached the end, we walked through the entire hallway, and he hadn't looked at the pictures once.

I hadn't realized our destination was on our right, the last door, the only entry in the hallway. Facing it, Jude gently turned the bronze vintage-looking knob, opening to a dark room.

We both stepped inside, feeling the wall for a light switch, which Jude found. As the light flickered on, I'm not going to lie; I was between pure confusion and laughter.

It was the size of a closet.

The light was dim.

This old-looking brown patterned wallpaper covered the walls.

The only decorative thing in the room was the light hanging from the low ceiling.

"Well, as you can see, my parents have a sick sense of humor," Jude released with a slightly irritated sigh.

There wasn't much space to look around, so I took a breather and leaned against the wall. Which would have gone smoothly if I had actually leaned against a wall.

Instead, right as I rested my back, the wall turned into a door, and I turned red from the embarrassment of falling on my back. I fell onto a small wooden floor, and inches away from my face was a step. As you may have guessed, this step had other step-siblings.

I don't care what anyone thinks; that was a good pun.

"Lucy!" Jude helped me up, and after gently doing so, we both looked up the staircase. Towards the top, you could see natural sunlight shining in. "A secret passageway, nice touch Mom and Dad,"

Jude turned to me with a cheesy grin. "Sherlock and Watson are back at it again; let's proceed!" We both ran up the steps without hesitation, skipping two at a time. When we reached the top platform getting hit with the sun's light, we took a right and were finally there.

Mission Complete.

6. Pocket Marbles 

Right away, I saw where the light was coming from; two giant windows were on the slanted wall as you entered. Windows you could walk through like a door when cranked out. If you stepped out of these windows, though, you would be on the roof, which had a killer view, I must say.

The ceiling was tall, and this room looked like a very well-renovated attic, a *gigantic attic.*

White walls with a light hardwood floor.

He had a red bike with white wall tires hanging up on a rack anchored to the wall.

For goodness sake, is that what I think it is-

"Lucy, oh my gosh," The both of us walking towards it, "I was completely kidding. I didn't think they would *actually* do this!"

We looked at each other likes kids waking up on Christmas morning.

"I believe you should go first, Miss Lucy."

With a smirk of giddiness, I couldn't resist.

It was a swing.

His parents installed a swing.

A swing that securely hung from the tall ceiling.

The wooden seat matched the floor, and the white cushion matched the sturdy ropes it hung down on.

Excitedly hopping up and grabbing hold of the ropes, I felt Jude's hands placed on my shoulders as he pulled me back and began to push me. It surprised me a little less each time his hands met my back, but after a while, I got distracted from looking around this room, his room.

I started to get higher up, and the small gust of wind hitting my face and rushing through my loose clothes was relieving, *like a breath of fresh air*, if you will.

Gosh, he had the coolest room I had ever seen.

A giant bookshelf filled with books, the bottom held his records, and there were little trinkets in some of the spaces.

It looks like he took most of his wall décor with him to Virginia because his walls here were pretty bare. Though it looked nice this way, the white walls radiated.

"Lucy!"

That sounded farther away than just behind me.

"I found it! Come here!"

Okay, he definitely wasn't behind me.

Turning my head around while my heels met the floor for a subtle halt, I looked to where his voice was calling. But I didn't see him. Just as I was about to give up and call back to ask where in the world he was, his voice echoed once more.

"Up here!"

And apparently, this room had a loft because what did it not have, right? There was a ladder hooked on some rails by wheels on the wall. I was tempted to ride it around the room rather than climb it, but I'm sure I'll have time for that later. Or I'd be sneaking in for that sole purpose.

Anyway, the sunlight from the loft caught my eyes while climbing up. I was squinting so much that they were practically shut. Even though it stung for a moment, they automatically opened when I heard the first notes of one of my favorite songs.

'Come on Eileen' by Dexys Midnight Runners.

Packed with so many memories, I was smiling already.

Finally getting my feet up on the floor, the brightness source came from the giant round window on the back wall. There wasn't that much space up here, but there was a bit of spaciousness to it. Both side walls came on a slant, and this window was so large that if I stood next to it, the thing would still have quite a bit of height on me.

Sad when a window is cooler than you.

There was only one object in the loft, not making it hard to deduce what this special item was, and I should have known.

Jude's beloved piano.

He acknowledged my presence, but his eyes didn't stray away from his keys.

The light captivated both of us, I think it's safe to say, into this wonderfully calm feeling. Like Jude didn't have his sister's wedding to help organize, and like I had never left home.

The bench he was sitting on was big enough for us, which I think he anticipated for me to join as he was scooted over to one side. Accompanying him, he smiled brightly at me. He did a fantastic piano key slide with his right hand, making me laugh and gearing him into extreme-passionate-musician mode. Within a few seconds, we had both reached close to max geekery level as we burst into song.

Surprisingly enough, I really didn't care that I was a lousy singer; who was I trying to impress, the window?

No, we didn't care at all, we were in our own separate rockin' worlds, and that was good. Sometimes you need an escape into your own little music world where you can sing every note perfectly. Every song that comes on, you just happen to be singing in front of an audience that thinks you're the most amazingly talented human being on this Earth. Or perhaps that's just me.

This upright piano is the most Jude thing I've ever seen.

The keys were splattered with light paint colors. The front of the piano was partially painted like *Vincent Van Gogh's The Starry Night,* and some of the painted twirling winds were musical notes. They didn't look like random notes, though. They looked like specific notes to a song.

On the corner of the front paneling, right in front of me, was a sticky note that appeared to be mod podge on the wood. It was kind of sloppy handwriting, and the words were fading, but it said, *'YOU got THIS.'*

I don't think I really needed to ask who wrote this; I had a feeling of who it was.

After realizing I had slowly stopped singing due to my self-exploration of this fricken superb piano, Jude had stopped and looked over it too.

Feeling the paint's dried ridges on his fingertips. When they reached the music notes, I asked about their significance, to which he explained he had been trying to figure that out for years.

"I actually didn't paint this, Julia, and-" I saw his eyes wander past the music notes and to the sticky note for a split second before picking up his sentence. "Someone else, did this. She won't tell me what song the notes are from. She claims I'm a *'Piano Master,'* and I should be able to figure it out."

Laughing with him, I asked, "But I don't see any sheet music, so you must be a Piano Master, being able to play a classic like that off the top of your head."

Putting up his hands in a playful surrender "You got me on the sheet music." As his arms came back down and rested on his lap, he turned to the round window. "That's a hell of a window, huh?"

"Yea," A small chuckle traveled with my answer. I just couldn't believe how big it was! "I wonder what it was like building this place and putting it in."

Jude turned to me momentarily, "You are a philosopher Lucy, don't forget it." He spoke in a melodramatic tone until he cracked a smile. One thing among the many silly things about Mr. Johnson is he can't pretend to be serious for long.

"Let's go check it out,"

I can't help but fall into that and his randomly spontaneous curiosity head first.

Jolting up, he tiptoed, ninja-super-agent-like, to the window.

Goodness, this reminded me of the night we went to *Lighthouse Island* for the first time, sneaking into Jude's own house while Carder was asleep.

Ah, good times, good times.

Looking out, we saw there was a balcony outside of the window. I could feel the uneasiness plastered on my face.

I'm not too big on balconies.

But never fear, *Sherlock Holmes* was here.

Jude moved a small latch on the side and gently pushed on the glass, and the thick glass circle moved; like a revolving door but, you know, not a revolving door.

I'm not good at explaining things, no points for me.

Climbing through the open space and onto this small balcony, it looked out to the pier I was by early today with Carder.

Oh Carder, I hope he's feeling better. It's a bit lame, but I miss him;

he would have some kind of remark or entertaining fascination with all the new things we discovered.

Jude was good company though, great even! But you can't compare and replace people's presence.

We admired the skyline out in the distance.

Gazed at all the trees, I will probably never get over.

And breathed in the refreshing air from the water riding along to us on the breeze.

We sat on the balcony floor, leaning against the guardrails.

I typically am not for this type of thrill.

But hey, I'm wild,

I can't be tamed.

Jude sat in one corner with his legs extended out, and I was in the other in the same position. I was looking through the cracks of the rails to the water, which reminded me of home when I felt something brush against my leg.

Looking down to see a marble next to me.

A marble?

I don't even remember the last time I saw a marble.

Assuming the owner, I looked at him, and he was already waiting with a goofy expression on his face for me to roll it back. Laughing under my breath, I did so.

The marble rolled back to me. "Should I ask where you got this, or believe your pockets generate marbles?" Rolling the marble back to him.

"Wouldn't that be something? Though, I don't know if I would want it to just be narrowed down to marbles."

The marble returned, stopping it with my finger. "If not marbles, then what?" Gently pushing it back.

"Pistachios"

Back,

"Ooohhh, but of course."

And fourth.

"But to answer your question, I *surprisingly* have no idea where this marble came from. I just reached into my pocket, and it was in there. Maybe I found it a while ago, pocketed it, and forgot."

"Or, you have a marble stealing problem."

"You know, Lucy, I think you're right. Please don't tell anyone; I know I have a problem. I can change!" His giggling plea was almost convincing.

"The first step to recovery is admitting you have a problem; we're making progress already!"

Ironically, he pocketed the marble, and we both went back inside.

I got my turn to ride on the moving wall ladder: Childhood dream complete. And Jude got his turn on the swing. He was pumping hardcore and definitely got higher than I did.

After our small spurts of cardio, I sat on the floor leaning against the piano while the Piano Master played.

I could feel the strings' vibration inside, hard at work to make the beautiful notes come to life. I would guess what song he played a few times, but most of this time, I closed my eyes and simply listened.

This little getaway was nice. I mean, we could easily do everything we were doing back home. But it meant something more here; it wasn't taken for granted; it was cherished into a memory.

With my eyes still closed, I felt a slight touch on my hand; I expected it to be Jude, but he wasn't there.

The music, it was still playing, though?

Lifting myself up off the floor to get a glance at the keys; they were still moving, their conductor missing, but the melody still quite alive.

Then again, I felt the same gentle touch on my shoulder. Turning around quickly in reaction to this surprise, I was, indeed, surprised.

"Colin?"

He smiled at me like he was happy and or he was surprised I remembered him.

"What're you-" But I wasn't sleeping? "What's going on?"

Maybe I am, but the music was still playing?

"Lucy, have you seen the trees here?! There's so many!" His enthusiasm made me forget for a second that this wasn't real.

As always, I'm dreaming. Just a dream and nothing more.

"I'll race you to the tallest one!"

Dream or not, though, there was no way I would pass up a chance to race and climb a tree with Colin.

I mean, he beat me there, but it didn't matter; it was still fun.

It seemed effortless for us to climb up; then again, we are pros.

We sat on a thick branch towards the top, me leaning against the tree and Colin facing me with some space between us and his legs on each side. The sun found its way through the leaves, giving us just enough light and warmth to not have to shield our eyes and not sweat. It's always a plus to not sweat.

"This place is beautiful, huh, Lucy?"

I nodded. "Yea," Embracing his smile and calmness while he was looking out at the other trees. "It is beautiful, Colin."

"Hey," He turned his head to me with a bright expression. "Wanna play the knocking game again? It's been forever!"

Geez, it has been forever.

One Knock= Yes

Two Knocks= No

I knocked once.

"Yes! Okay, um, oh! Remember Dad's homemade bread?"

Laughing, I knocked once.

"Figured you would, seeing it's the best bread in the universe. Not even just in this world, in any world, even if they don't know what bread is, which would be such a sad thing; it's the best bread."

Such a dork for bread.

"Okay, okay, your turn, judgmental-bread-hater."

"Oh stop, I am not; you're just a bread enthusiast."

"What better way to be?"

Both of us giggled after I waved it off. "Do you remember how Mom and Dad used to dance together when they thought we weren't watching?"

With a broad smile, he knocked once. "Gosh, do I ever. They made being in love look as easy as breathing in and out. I swear they fell in love with each other over and over again all the time."

I thought about the last phone call I had with Dad; I should give him a call soon to see how he and Mom are doing.

Mom,

I'm so worried about her.

I want to ask if Colin knows if she's doing okay, but the answer is just going to be what I want to hear. I'm the one dreaming all of this up, my subconscious, or whatever.

Too much thinking; this is making my head hurt.

Colin's voice broke through my chaotic dreaming thoughts. "It was so natural for the both of them. Every step they took never looked out of place. They really set the bar high for our love expectations," He laughed and carried on. "I'm pretty sure Dad was a realist until he met Mom. And now he's a hopeless romantic who lives and breathes to make his family happy, and for the next moment he gets to dance with Mom."

My head cocked up at his last words. "You really think they'll always be together Colin?"

One knock.

Releasing a soft laugh, "Seriously though?"

"Well, yea, of course. Why? Do you doubt it?"

Two knocks. "I know they really truly love each other. I'm just scared that something will happen to one of them one day. I don't know. I worry too much."

One knock from Colin.

"Oh, shut up with that."

Laughing, he scooted a bit closer. "You've got nothing to worry about, Lucy. Mom is going to be A-Okay."

But I didn't say anything-

"She and Dad went on quite the romantic date," With a goofy raise of his eyebrows. "They went to the art museum, which I'm sure they've gone to a dozen times, but those hippies love it, all the same. After that, they went out to eat and ordered dessert first like badasses, and I think later-"

Colin stopped talking,

I grew confused;

We both heard my name.

But shortly after my name was repeated,

We knew what was happening.

Colin looked at me with glossy eyes, his face was strained, and he was just hardly shaking his head in disbelief.

His smile was absent, replaced with a trembling bottom lip. Usually, his smile tries to hang on and linger for as long as possible; it had completely checked out.

Someone was waking me up, and I was slowly leaving the dream.

"Lucy," Colin's eyes looked back and forth between mine, looking for something. "No, please," looking for more time, "I'm not ready to go yet" again.

I felt a sharp pain in my throat, like I couldn't catch my breath. "Coli-"Reaching for his hand, I woke up. Jude's hand was placed on mine, trying to politely wake me up.

7. Don't Go Changing

"**H**eeyyy sleepy Jean,"

I wanted to reflect Jude's smile, but I was still lost in my dream.

"I'm sorry I woke you up. You fell asleep, so I carried you over here, and you're actually the first person to sleep in my bed; it's new! Anyway, you fell asleep, so I sat you on the bed and went back downstairs to help Julia. She's back, and so is everyone else, including the De'Amores!"

I think he was waiting for an enthusiastic reaction, so I gave him the best smile I could express at the moment, which seemed to be enough for him.

"I don't know if you know how long you've been out, but it's nine o'clock now."

Now I had a wide-eyed, partly open-mouth expression.

He was amused. "It's okay! It's totally fine; I wanted to come to say goodbye though because me, Julia, and I'm not sure if the other bridesmaids are going, but we have to go out for a traditional whatever bridesmaid's night out thingy."

I still couldn't get over the fact he was the maid of honor.

"Yea keep smirking there," Jude said in a sarcastic but harmless tone. "Will you be alright?"

Giving him a strange look at first, I quickly replaced it with a convincing grin. "Jude, yes, of course, don't worry." The believable grin has won yet again. "Have you seen Carder out and about?"

"Oh! Yea! Yes, yes, I have. He's actually hanging out with Angelo's cousins. You should totally go join them; they'd love you!" His excitement made me smile and drift away from the dream I had just left.

I loved seeing Colin in my dreams.

Really, I do.

But I hate saying goodbye every time.

Over and over again.

"I'll probably do that," Giving Jude a nod and sitting up more. "I'm going to give my parents a call first. Is it okay if I make the call in here?"

He gave me a *'scolding'* look, "Lucy, you don't have to ask. Of course, you can."

"Okay, okay, thank you, I'm just so comfy right now."

And with a laugh,

A smile,

And a knuckle touch goodbye;

He was off on his girl's night out.

And I dialed my parent's number, waiting through the dial tone.

I perked up when I heard the phone clicking on the other end.

"Ground control to Major Father; come in."

"This is Major Father to ground control!"

I know I'm the one who started the joke, but Dad always has a way of making it funnier. "Hello there, how's your day going?"

I could hear something in the background, it was faint, but it must have been loud over by him. "Is Mom there?"

There was a delay in his answer. "Huh? Oh yes! She is waiting for me on the dance floor; we're living, Traveler!"

Dad and Mom are out *dancing*?

"How's New York?!"

What in the world is happening? "Exciting, very exciting; your day sounds much more entertaining though, let's hear it!"

"Alright, well, I surprised your Mom with a nice planned-out day. First, we went for a stroll around the Art Museum. We talked about our favorite paintings, and we have a few pictures of each other trying to pose like the person in the painting we're standing in front of."

Oh Lord, those darn quirky rebels. I'll never question where Colin and I got our weirdness from.

"Then we went to a restaurant your Mom and I wanted to try out, and we thought, *'You know what, heck with it, we're living on the edge today!'* and we ordered dessert first."

Wait, what?

"And now we are working off the calories at this interesting Dance Club-there are so many lights. I'm glad we came here on their *'Oldies Music'* night. I would have no idea how to dance to the sounds that are popular these days!"

Colin told me that, the restaurant thing, in my dream. And he was about to tell me something else before I woke up.

"I don't want to leave your Mom waiting too long; someone might steal her, you know; she's the best catch!"

How could he have known? My subconscious, that is, Colin couldn't have really told me?

"Can Mom and I call you tomorrow? I'm sorry I have to check out so soon; I feel our roles are reversed now."

My mind froze for a moment before I shook my thoughts and answered, "Yea, I'd love to; it may have to be early, though because of the wedding."

"Yes! Yes, of course! I can't wait to hear about your journey. Send our hellos to Carder! I love you, and so does Mom, Traveler. We love you so much."

"Dad," Speaking in a touched, sentimental voice. "I love you guys too. I'm excited to hear how the rest of your night goes and see those Art Gallery pictures."

Sharing a laugh, I pulled the phone away to hang up until I heard him call me back as I put it back to my ear.

"Yes?"

"Thank you for your support on everything happening with your Mother lately. I know you have a lot on your plate, and I appreciate it so very much."

"You don't have to thank me, Dad-"

"She's glowing, Lucy, gosh, she's shining. I haven't seen her smile like that in what feels like forever. Whenever your Mom smiles, ever since I met her, it's released this endorphin; but it's not just any chemical Traveler. No, it's one that's been hidden inside this old brain my whole life, and it was never triggered until she smiled at me. Today it hit me like a sack of records. I couldn't stop looking at her and reminding myself how lucky I am to have such a beautiful human being in my life."

That little speech reminded me of our rock-skipping sessions on the beach. Gosh, how I missed it; I craved it even more now.

"Look at me, reciting a novel. Thank you for listening to me again." Dad paused.

I could hear the sound in the background growing a little louder. "I love you, Lucy. Stay safe, okay?"

"Always, Dad."

"And Lucy?"

"Yes?"

"Don't go changing on me."

There was that inaudible sound of his smile; I hope I never ever forget that smile.

Leaving Jude's bedroom was like leaving his little world and entering New York City all over again.

I actually didn't really want to leave the room,

With how peaceful it was in there;

But I really wanted to see how Carder was holding up.

I turned the corner of the hallway outside Jude's secret door and ran into someone, which scared the living shit out of me. They had me by the shoulders in reaction to bumping into each other and preventing me from falling.

It was a guy,

Around my age-ish,

I'm going to take a wild guess that this is one of Angelo's cousins,

And handsome runs in the family.

"Are you, Lucy?"

Holy buckets, his accent, I could listen to him all day. Literally, I would let him talk all day. But I was still a bit taken aback by his question. Clearing my throat softly, "Um, yes, I am?" Trying to keep it short so I don't say something stupid.

Let's be honest,

I have a knack for doing that.

But I didn't say something stupid this time,

Nope,

I apparently said something that made this guy extremely overjoyed.

For he cheered after yelling, '*L'ho trovata! I found her!*',

Picked me up,

Threw me over his shoulder,

And sprinted down the hall.

I was going to scream,

But in all honesty,

I was way too lazy for that vocal exercise.

I know, I know,

If I was in a life-or-death situation, I'd be screwed.

But I'm not,

Well, I hope not.

I have no idea.

He had sprinted well across the house and down the stairs. To answer your question, yes, that was quite brutal on the stomach.

Angelo's cousin finally put me down.

Where I was met with quite a few other people,

Music,

Some of them had red cups in their hands,

I had been brought to a party.

So, I was wrong,

This was death.

I was going to confront the guy who brought me here, but he was long gone. So, I decided to do what I do best in these situations; wander.

I wandered and wandered until I walked into a room. Quite a crowded room with a Ping-Pong table in the middle.

And lo and behold, standing at the end of it was Carder himself.

Ping-Pong?

Did he really play that?

I had no idea he played.

And in that second, we made eye contact.

I wasn't sure what his reaction to seeing me would be, but I was thrilled with the one I got. Waving me over excitedly, I excused myself through the small crowd around the table and reached him.

"You're just in time to see me kick this fella's ass,"

"Si sta per perdere figlio di una cagna!" Carder's opponent yelled from across the table. He was jumping in place, *'getting warmed up.'* He seemed pretty competitive.

"Yea, yea, keep the comments coming! It only fuels me!" Carder shouted back.

I think he's the one who's going to get his ass kicked.

All the sudden, the guy who ran me in here shouted to Carder while running into the room, "He said, *'You are going to lose you son of a bitch!'*" Ending the translation, he ran out and into the party again.

"Oh, oh hey! You found Lucy!" Carder yelled back at the guy.

You could faintly hear his response, "Yes I did!" He must have super-sonic hearing.

Carder's opponent tapped his ping-pong paddle on the table to get Carder's attention. Once that worked, he gestured to the table. As if to say, *'Are we going to play or what, pretty boy?'*

8. Intertwined Shadows 

Of course, I've heard of ping-pong, but I've never really seen it played in front of me. Backing up like the rest of the people in the room, I noticed the floor was littered with scattered ping-pong balls.

Both of them set their paddles down on the end of the table with the handle facing towards them. The guy, whose name I really need to learn so I can stop calling him guy, on the end, tossed the ball *Michael Jordan* style in the air. The ball barely missed the paddle on Carder's side, and disappointment filled that half of the room.

I put together that the goal was to see who would hit the paddle first, and whoever did would get to serve?

And followed by that and some cheering on Carder's side, my theory was correct.

I was actually learning quite a bit!

Like:

You play to 21 points,

The term *'teardrop'* means the ball falls to the ground before hitting it.

And when Someone says, *'Let's Volley,'* that means let's get started or let's play.

Damn, I'm getting cooler by the minute being here.

This game may have been the most intense competition I have seen. I was listening to the conversations around me, and it turned out that there was a Ping-Pong Tournament when I was asleep. The final two were Carder and the guy whose name turned out to be Lucca.

The name suited him pretty well.

He was nicely dressed.

Facial structure was on point.

And he held his head high.

He was the kind of person you wanted to get approval from, but they also would be scary as all hell if you ended up on their bad side.

With the score at 18 to 9, Carder was inching his way to the bad side.

But Carder could have cared less what anyone in this room thought; he was in the zone.

As Carder served, the intenseness continued with occasional unnecessary grunts from each of them. Someone shouted, *'Angelo, you bastard, get over here!'* Turning to where the yell was coming from, I saw the guy who carried me down slapping Angelo on the back, and they both laughed.

I wanted to go talk to them for the purpose of:

1. To find out that guy's fricken name

2. Congratulate Angelo and get to know him

But there was no way I could just nonchalantly walk over there. I mean, come on, they are speaking Italian right now; you know how awkward it would be if I walked over there and pretended I knew what they were saying.

I'd just keep nodding

and smiling,

while they joke about this dumb American girl who thinks she can pull a fast one on two clever men.

While this scenario was playing through my head, to my surprise, they were walking my way; smiles and all.

The social anxiety.

I repeat:

THE SOCIAL ANXIETY.

I recognized Angelo closer up from the picture Julia showed me at the hospital; goodness gracious, they are so adorable. And as the two men approached me and began a conversation that quickly went in the direction of Angelo's beautiful fiancé, you could tell from the tone of his voice, the spark in his eyes, and the words he chose- he was totally and completely in love with her.

The chat ranged from everything to wedding cake to arguing over which restaurant was better back in their hometown. And that led to each of them trying to convince me theirs was the best restaurant in Italy; I have to admit it was pretty hysterical.

Oh, and the guy who threw me on his shoulder eventually introduced himself and apologized for the abrupt abduction. His name is Amadore, and he is Lucca's brother and Angelo's cousin.

Angelo has many, many cousins.

I'm pretty jealous.

I always wondered what it'd be like to have such a big family.

To know that you have a relative to fall back on.

"He hasn't been bothering you too much, I hope," Angelo directed towards me but was discreetly looking to poke some fun at his cousin.

Amadore was the silly cousin. If everything that has happened tonight hasn't covered that. But before I could assure Angelo he wasn't a bother, Amadore proved me wrong.

"Please, we're practically an item."

Angelo and I exchanged looks.

Mine was amusement with a mix of embarrassment.

His was disgust and irritation like he had heard this before.

"Don't hide your feelings," Delivering a sly wink to me and then turning to Angelo, "And I've already *picked her up.*"

We had to surrender to that pun; that was pretty punny.

Luckily all the wild cheering from Carder's victory gave me the perfect opportunity to tell them it was nice meeting them. Once I received their polite smiles, I ran to congratulate Carder.

Man, was this place a riot!

Everyone was laughing,

Some chats were in Italian,

Some English,

But everyone was super pumped about the Ping-Pong tournament.

"Lucy!" Carder swept me up, spun me in a circle, and set me down. It must be the adrenalin from being a Ping-Pong champion. "I don't even know what came over me! It was exhilarating! It was, it was insane!"

In all his excitement, his hands were wrapped around my shoulders, and his voice was hella loud trying to talk over all the noise, but I couldn't stop laughing and getting just as psyched about his win.

"It was the game point, sweat dripping down my forehead, Lucy, I hate to sweat, but I didn't care. I let that baby roll down like a close-up boxing movie scene. Anyway, I whack that ball over to his side, he hit it right back, I hit it back, well we hit it back and forth a lot, but then it was bouncing back to me and Lucy this superpower surged through my arm, and I smacked that fricken ball and Lucca missed it, he missed it! He blinked! He literally blinked, Lucy, he blinked, and he missed the ball; I HIT THE BALL WITH SO MUCH FORCE I BROKE THE LAWS OF TIME AND SPACE AND ANY OTHER SCIENCE! I BROKE IT ALL, LUCY! IT'S BROKEN, AND NO ONE CAN FIX IT!"

I was laughing so hard I was surprised his hands didn't fall off my shoulders. I cupped my hands around Carder's warm, and as of right now, childlike wonder face and spoke loudly and clearly to him.

"Carder, I no speak sports, BUT WAY TO GO, YOU KICKED SOME PING-PONG AND SCIENCE ASS!"

"Yes! Thank you! I am very tired!"

After joining in for a laugh, we said our goodnights to whomever we passed on our way out and started to make our way to the cottage house. Where Carder had already brought our stuff to our room.

What a gent, I tell ya.

Our room door had our names on a tapped piece of paper.

This place just got classier. And it was pretty darn adorable, I must admit.

The room was nice,

Lovely, even.

There were two beds,

A decent-sized bathroom.

This room, in particular, had a Sailboat Lighthouse kind of theme.

According to Carder, all the rooms had a different theme.

And, to Carder, this was the 'least tacky.'

I don't even know what's considered tacky and what's not.

Whatever, I like the room, and there's a bed.

I'm golden.

"Early day tomorrow Lucy-Luo."

Turning to him from my bed where my suitcase was, "Yes, early but adorable." Giving him a smile and turning back to the bed until I remembered something. "Oh! Mom and Dad send their love and hellos."

Carder put his hand to his heart and made a long '*Awwwww*' sound. "Those blessed people, they are gems I don't deserve. And you, my Dear, are the diamond."

"Oh, stop," I sassily replied, but of course, I was touched. "I'm not a diamond; you are."

"Honey, I'm not a diamond," He turned to me with emphasis. "I'm the motha fricken *Hope Diamond*."

I laughed as Carder told me he wasn't joking. Which only made me laugh more as I grabbed my pajamas and changed in the bathroom while Carder changed in the room.

After getting changed, I knocked, unlike some people, and entered the room to see him under the blanket.

Of my bed.

With his head poking out.

"You need to eat more. I wouldn't have known you were under there if it wasn't for your head."

"Lies" He looked over the bit of blanket covering his neck to see and then looked back to me. "Have I always been this way?"

"I'm afraid so." Taking a seat on the bed next to him, "I'm afraid you have Megaflatness."

"That was pathetic."

I drew back just a tad in *'offense'* "For being right on the spot, I think I make a damn good disease generator."

Carder giggled but still didn't move.

I gave him a nudge. "So why is the Ping-Pong champion soaking up his glory in my bed?"

Taking a moment to nestle even more into the bed, he responded after releasing a relaxed sigh. "I wanted to spend my first night in the Big Apple having a deep cliché night talk with my best friend."

There was no way I could say no to that.

I turned on the bedside lamp, shaped like a sailboat, and shut the lights off. Then, climbed under the blankets and followed Carder's lead of going completely under the covers.

"Are we five again?" I teased as I turned on my side, trying to get comfortable.

"Oh, come on, the way the lamp light shines through the blanket looks cool."

"So, indeed, we are five?"

I'll say I deserved it, but Carder pushed my arm supporting my head, and I took a small dive into my pillow; these wrists need a workout.

"Alright, alright, what shall we talk about?"

Carder's eyes drifted to the side in thought, and his smile came with it as they wandered back. "Let's just ask each other questions unless you have something specific to talk about?"

"I don't believe I do, but hmmm, let's see. When did you learn to play Ping-Pong?"

"Oh! I feel like I'm getting my first exclusive after winning the championship. I first started playing when I was eight. I used to play up until I was ten, then I gave it up for school Musicals. Which is when I think my Dad completely began to hate me. My Mom hated me ever since I started dressing myself. Which was as soon as I could reach the hangers in my closet. Dear Lord, that woman, and her malnourished fashion."

I was glad that ended on somewhat of a funny note. That made me think about Carder and his parents again. I wasn't sure if I should bring it up or not, though. I think it's still too touchy for tonight.

"What's an object you hate?"

I thought on that for a moment, then recalled the creepy timekeeper in our old Band class. "I am not a huge fan of metronomes, and you?"

Carder quickly rebutted. "That doesn't count as a question. You're odd. But my answer is tinsel. I hate tinsel."

"I know it doesn't technically count. I was just curious. And I'm odd? You love confetti; what's the difference between that and tinsel?"

By the roll of his eyes, I could tell already I was in for an impromptu Tedtalk. "Confetti has its cons, it's not always the greatest thing, but tinsel is just awful. It gets all over, there is no clear way of getting rid of it, and it lingers for months! I just hate it."

"Well, I better ask a question; this seems like a sensitive subject." There definitely was playful sass in my voice, but he wasn't having it. Mr. Grumpy Anti-Tinsel.

"If you could go back to any moment in time like whenever you were having a bad day and needed a break, you could go back to this specific moment; what would it be?"

"I don't know if I have a specific memory,"

As I was about to tell Carder there were no exceptions and he had to pick, he beat me to it.

"Wait! Yes, I have one- That scorching day a few years ago when the three of us brought a thing of sidewalk chalk, and we went around town writing either inspirational or funny quotes in weird places, drawing little people in their own little sidewalk world, or that one drawing all of us pitched in on, and it took a good twenty minutes. Remember that? It was just a giant black hole, and we took a picture of Colin pretending to fall into it. Oh my gosh, his whole body was in complete falling mode, and then his face was just straight at the camera, terrified but funny as ever."

Carder was caught up in the memory, and I was catching up and smiling while he was narrating. We never had to ask Colin to take a funny picture; he always volunteered.

"I miss him."

Carder's words cut right into my thoughts; looking at him, he looked down.

"I miss him, and I wish he could see this place."

I wish he would look at me.

"I've always wanted to tell you that I miss him, but I don't want you to think I'm trying to take him away from you or something. I don't know." Slowly, he tilted his head up, "I'm sorry."

Atta boy, thank you.

"I just murdered the vibe."

"Carder, I'm sorry if I gave off that impression-"

"No, no, you didn't. Don't worry about it."

As Carder looked back down again, I decided this would be his time. His time to grieve, in a sense. He was always the strong one for me; thank God for that.

"Maybe we should talk about Colin?"

Carder's head popped up. "Like, things we miss about him?"

Automatically, I smiled at the thought of that, "Yea, I like that idea,"

Carder smiled too. "I miss when he would narrate what you were doing until you noticed. I remember one time he got me for almost half an hour."

I laughed as I recalled that mischievous trait of his. Colin used to do that to Mom while she was cooking.

"Remember how much he loved hot chocolate? It could be 95 degrees out, and he would order a hot chocolate without hesitation."

"And if there was a movie involved, everyone was going to drink hot chocolate with him"

I felt my smile grow even bigger. "Yes!" Pointing like his statement was in the air and laughing, "At least he put marshmallows in them, though."

"OoooOooo yeees, those were delicious," Licking his lips like a dork. "Colin always wanted to watch a movie."

"I miss speaking in stupid voices with him at the most random times too. Like one time, we were in Church, and he leaned over and whispered something in a pirate voice, and I started laughing during the Pastor's sermon; that was fun to explain."

"I think I remember you telling me about that!"

As we reminisced in our laughter, I knew it was Carder's turn, but I had one more to say. "I remember when he used to say I miss you when he would be sitting right next to you."

I wasn't looking at Carder when I said this. I looked at the sheet the lamp's light shined down on and the slight shadow my fingers cast.

"Carder?"

My emotions were faster than the strength I had left in my vocal cords as the sadness latched itself on. It was beginning to feel almost overwhelming.

"I'm afraid I'm going to forget his voice." Who am I trying to fool? "And one day, it'll become one of these, one of these casted and once in a while retrieved memories we miss, but it'll slip away because it's inevitable, but I don't want it to be."

This topic will always be unbearably overwhelming. That was the inevitability I've always tried to cover up. "For once, I'd like to be strong and lucky enough to beat the odds."

Carder swiftly slipped his hand underneath mine, our shadows intertwined. "Look at me."

At his command, I looked. I looked into kind eyes that I knew would understand, but in a way, I didn't want them to. I wanted this to be my pain. I didn't want it to be this universal pain everyone understood.

"Look at the odds you have beat just laying here. Look how lucky you are right now."

But this isn't the Lucy show. This isn't a rare side effect of human loss or an emotion no one on this Earth has ever witnessed.

"You are in New York; you faced your fear of leaving your town. Hell, you've got a lot to be proud of!"

I needed to get a grip.

"I know for a fact Colin would be so damn proud of you right now. Please know that."

It's time to change the channel.

I sighed in the relief of getting those inner thoughts off my chest and pushing the gulping tears down, "What would I do without you, Dear Carder?"

He lightly lifted my hand to him as he kissed it, gently putting it down while uncovering the blankets from our heads, letting the rush of fresh air hit us, and looked at me. He looked at me straight on while his arm was extended back towards the lamp, "You don't have to worry about that, Lucy-Lou."

The lamp clicked off. The dark flooded out the last of its small radius of light. Leaving only just a slight outline of Carder's face, in which I could see a subtle but tired smile.

9. Fancy–Dancy© 

"Hellooo" I managed to scrap a groggy good morning out of my tired throat.

"Why helloooo there, sleeeeepy," Dad laughed as I heard the familiar fumbling routine of figuring out the speaker button on the phone. "You're on the air!"

Giggling and slowly becoming more awake, I sat up. "Let me put you on the air for your sleepy audience." With less of a struggle, I also put my phone on speaker. "How'd the rest of your night go, you crazy kids?"

Waiting for a response, I turned to see Carder climbed into his own bed last night, probably after I crashed. He was curled under his blankets, head and all, and I could hear a soft groan come from him; which I translated to:

'Go ahead, try to get me up, see what happens. SEE. WHAT. HAPPENS.'

"It was pretty spectacular! Your Mother and I haven't danced like that in ages. Literally, I don't even know what you guys dance like these days."

Laughing at my Dad automatically categorizing me with human beings who can actually dance, I swung my feet over the edge of the bed. Cringing just a tad when they met the cold floor. "Well, I'm glad you guys had fun; you most certainly deserve it."

"Hi, Honey!" Mom's voice chimed in, a bit high-pitched and giddy.

"Your Mother says Hi!"

As I was about to laugh again, I heard Dad say something back to my Mom and now back to me.

"So, how are you and Carder doing this wonderful Sunday morning?"

"Good, good" I felt the mischievous smile come across my face just as the idea was already going in motion. "Oh, why," Standing up and seeing Carder's figure move a little from curiosity, "Carder is actually up and about as we speak!"

Now this made Carder's bedhead pop out from the blanket and pierce me with his eyes, which once again said something along the lines of

'I swear, you do this to me, and this will be your last Sunday.'

Whelp,

Happy Last Sunday!

As I climbed onto the bed and began jumping around him, he stood his ground and stayed covered.

I think Dad was catching on. "Your Mother and I send our good mornings to him!"

Amongst my jumping, I heard Carder's muffled 'Good morning' from under the blanket.

"He says good morning too!" I chirped as I took the call off speaker phone. I said I love you and goodbye to Dad and Mom and hung up the phone to begin the day.

The big day.

"Carder." Unshyly slamming myself on the bed, landing on my back next to him, "It's the wedding day; how can you not be ecstatic right now?!"

Finally, he unmasked himself from the fluffy blanket. "I am ecstatic, you're just excessively ecstatic, so it's clouding my excitement. Can't you see how excited I am?"

Mind you, this was all spoken in one tone. A tone that could have been easily mistaken for a person on their death bed.

"I will tickle you," I knew this should spark something; there's not a soul over eight who likes to be tickled. Especially Carder's cranky soul.

His head jerked towards me. "Tickle me, you die."

Putting my hands up in a *'tickle threatening'* way, "Get up, get up, get up!"

"Lucccyyyy, it's too early for this shenanigans bullshit."

Sighing as I put my hands down because as much as I want it to be a happy Sunday, I'm not searching for a last Sunday. I plopped myself back down; dramatically.

"For the sake of adorable matrimony and formal outfits, I will get up and make myself fabulous."

"You mean even more fabulous than you look already?" Trying my best not to let my grin break through my straight face.

It was an admirable attempt, at least.

"Oh, don't start with me" His stray hairs stood straight up and moved with the motions of his head. Before getting up, Carder turned on his side to me as I did the same.

"Game plan: I use this bathroom; you use the one in the hallway because the shower is nicer. Are you doing your own hair?"

"I was just going to wear it down."

"Okay, so I'm going to do your hair, so you go shower and whatnot, and I'll do the same."

After both of us chanted BREAK, we clapped and sprung out of bed, each of us going our separate directions.

And man, oh man,

Was this hallway bathroom nice.

No.

Luxurious.

This was a luxurious bathroom.

This bathroom is nicer than our entire apartment.

Perhaps there will be two weddings today.

Because I,

Lucy May MacArthur,

Have fallen in love.

Of course, I'm joking.

I only have eyes for *Mr. Cumberbatch.*

But back to this bathroom.

The shower was *huge.*

If I was coordinated enough to do a cartwheel, I could do one in this shower; it was *that* big.

I was mesmerized as I was getting ready for my first-ever extravagant shower. There are jets in this shower. I don't have to stand in one place under a showerhead, I can literally stand anywhere in there, and I will get fancy-dancy-clean!

Fancy-dancy,

What a lovely word,

I could dance while I get clean,

In a fancy shower.

That's my word:

Fancy-dancy©

Before I could get fancy-dancy© clean, though, I needed to actually turn the shower on. Which I had no idea how.

Wrapping myself in a wonderfully soft towel, I planned to sneak across the hallway and ask Carder if he knew how to work this thing.

But of course,

Like most of my plans,

It did not go as envisioned in my head.

I saw myself tip-toeing ninja-like to our room.

Carder would make some smartass comment about my inability to figure out how the shower works. And then he wouldn't be able to figure out how the glorious shower works. But then, while watching him fumble around trying to get it to work, I would figure out how to turn it on, and I would get a point.

This is not at all how it went down.

I will receive no points.

I intended to get to the room as fast as possible, the moment I opened the door, I charged out. And instantly, I collided with another plan that did not go how it was, I assume, intended.

In a whip and a flash, I found myself on the ground from the impact of the other busy human. Thank God I was still securely wrapped in the towel, but I was not thankful for the person also lying on the floor that fell as well.

Damnit, fricken rhyming again.

Looking away from me while talking, "Wow! Good morning!" Along with a nervous chuckle, "I'm terribly sorry. I was going to pop in to see if you and Carder needed anything."

I then realized he wasn't looking at me because he didn't know if my towel had fallen off. "Good morning to you too, Sir, and my towel is still on Jude," Laughing at his blushing face, he turned to me. "Oh! Maybe I could have your assistance if you aren't busy?"

Standing up as he did, too. "I can't get the shower to turn on."

Of course, he got it on right away. Some button was well camouflaged with the tile on the wall. I gave him a slow and maybe sassy clap.

To which he did a slow bow with a tad of sass. "Sometimes fancy is hard, unnecessarily hard."

"Thank you, I am excited to use this fancy shower!"

"Oh, okay."

Jude and I turned to the open doorway, where we saw Carder speaking sharply with his hands on his hips.

"So it's okay for him to go in the shower, but when Carder does it, *it's not okay and not normal.*"

Without either of us having time to give Carder an explanation, he walked away. And without me giving Jude an explanation, he awkwardly laughed again and walked to Carder.

So, that happened.

But on the bright side, that shower was absolutely amazing.

Upon entering the bedroom, my outfit for the day was placed on my bed, and Carder was still in the bathroom getting ready.

This dress was gorgeous; I hadn't seen it before. After discovering the price tag was still on it, I put together Carder had bought it.

He has excellent taste in dresses. It was a short, about knee length, with a pale, almost washed out lilac color, lace dress.

I couldn't wait to slip into it. Its inside cloth layer made the dress not itchy from the lace, which I was worried about, and I had my black flats waiting for me on the floor.

As I stepped into them, the bathroom door quietly opened, and out stepped Carder.

Torso: The same pale lilac color, long sleeve dress shirt.

Accessories: White paisley bow tie.

Bottom half: Black slacks, his dress shirt tucked in, of course.

Shoes: Black dress shoes.

A perfect match;

Our outfits that is.

I'm assuming Jude explained the earlier situation to Carder since he didn't bring it up; I'm hoping Carder said nothing about our previous 'shower incidents.'

"Lucy-Lou," His giddy smile, "You look undeniably beautiful."

It wasn't his words that made me feel somewhat beautiful, and it wasn't this gorgeous dress; it was that damn smile.

"Nice touch, huh?" Gesturing to my outfit and his.

Gazing down at my dress before nodding to him, "You do have a knack for that." I couldn't help but beam at the two of us, two lilac peas in a pod.

We walked into the bedroom's bathroom so Carder could fix my hair; in his words, it was *Medusa's wannabe sister's monstrous hairdo.*

Gotta love that guy.

Quickly, but might I say beautifully, he pinned my hair up in this fancy-looking bun.

I couldn't even begin to copy it if he took it all down and said, 'Okay, here now you do it.'

"Alright," Carder spoke, breaking my spacing out thoughts. "Go ahead and look at my amazing work."

And that it was, as I looked up into the mirror. I kind of did feel beautiful. A smile reflected me in the mirror as my eyes peeled away to Carder's, who I caught smiling at me.

Carder took a slight step back and overlooked me, turning me towards him, then returned his bright grin to mine. "We are all set. Now, let's go cry our eyes out at some disgustingly romantic perfect love!"

Laughing while he gently took my arm and hooked it around his, he escorted us out of the cottage, and to our amazement, the grounds were flooded with people.

Fancily dressed people, I wonder if they got fancy-dancy© this fine Sunday morning.

I really need to contact whoever is in charge of words.

The Word Wizards.

Because this is gold.

Seriously though, there were so many people here. However, I couldn't have imagined it any less with how spectacular both of these wonderful people are. Oh my gosh, I can't wait to see them get married.

It was kind of fun to be in this crowd of people. Fitting in but not being recognized and smiling at other people's laughter, because how could you not be happy on such a beautiful day for love?

We made our way to where the ceremony would take place, a great open space in the garden where white wooden foldable chairs were already set up. Carder squeezed my arm a little out of pure giddy excitement. Which resulted in us turning to each other, giggling like well-dressed morons, hushing each other, and then trying to find our seats quietly.

Not many people were already in their seats; I don't think the ceremony started for at least another half hour. Then again, we are some pretty lazy intro-verts.

"I wonder what cake they'll be serving," Carder said, looking straight ahead like he was lost in a cake fantasy.

"So that's what you're thinking about right now?"

Carder turned to me for just a moment for his remark, "Oh, don't act like you aren't thinking of it too," and then he returned to his distant stare.

Of course, I couldn't deny this. "Yea, alright," cake is always somehow on my mind. "But I'm more excited for the vows."

"I am going to be a mess; I completely blanked on that."

"You forgot about the vows, possibly the most romantic part of the wedding besides the actual '*I do's*?"

"I'm thinking about cake! Don't blame me; blame the cake!"

"How am I supposed to properly blame it if I don't even know what flavor it is?!"

At this point, the elderly people enjoying this quiet, lovely space with us left to enjoy another atmosphere. One that didn't involve young adults arguing over cake that wasn't theirs.

After the *'oh so heated argument'* ended, it was cut off by a vibration coming from Carder's pocket.

That got him a small punch in the arm.

He mouthed *'Owch'* while reaching for his phone to read the text message.

"I thought we agreed to leave our phones in the room?"

"Well," turning the phone towards me, "It's a good thing I didn't."

JudeBro: *"Meet me in the front NOW. HURRY."*

Jude may not know this at the moment, but he just made two very lazy introverts sprint in fancy clothes.

Once we reached Jude, he brought a finger to his lips, signaling us to be quiet, then waving for us to follow him.

Now I feel like the spy-ninja I knew I was born to be.

Alright,

Perhaps not,

But it felt badass.

Jude led us to a different part of the cottage's property; from there, we hid behind some bushes.

Quietly, Jude smiled and whispered to us, "I'm not positive if this is where it's going to happen, but I just have a feeling. And I knew you guys would probably love to see this, so I brought you here, and by the way, you both look quite nice this morn-"

"Jude," Carder softly muttered.

"Right, sorry" He pointed to this giant, beautiful willow tree that wasn't too far away from us. "I think it's going to happen there. I know Julia loves that tree. When we used to talk on the phone while I was in Virginia, she always told me she was talking to me while sitting under it."

"What's going to happen, though?" Carder asked impatiently.

"Right! So, it's pretty universal that the bride and groom aren't supposed to see one another before the wedding. They aren't going to see each other. Julia always loved those pictures online of couples who would write a little note to each other before the wedding and meet somewhere secret to exchange them. But they'll be on a different side of the tree, so they won't see each other."

While he explained this, Jude looked at the tree, smiling, like he'd envisioned it all while the words came out.

"That was well worth the wait for an explanation Jude. If this is the spot, which I dearly hope it is now, Lucy and I are going to dramatically die from cuteness overexposure all over these conveniently placed bushes."

I was about to laugh when the three of us suddenly heard something and fell silent as we peeked sneakily through the bushes.

Julia was in her wedding dress, and I was speechless. Completely speechless.

She looked so graceful, like an oil painting in a storybook about a beautiful woman awaiting to meet her beloved soulmate. Her smile, just her altogether, was glowing.

The tree trunk was so large it was a perfect place to hide and secretly be found. Julia stayed behind one side of the tree, never peeking or anything. I nearly gasped as I saw Angelo approaching from the opposite side, looking very dapper indeed in his tux and standing with his back against the tree.

We couldn't hear what they were saying as they slipped each other their own little notes, and in a way, I liked not knowing. They deserved to have that to themselves. We were being nosey enough.

Angelo reached for Julia's hand as they kept whispering, never seeing one another with their backs still to the tree. For the remainder of their short, secret meeting, they held hands like there was nothing else worth letting go for in the world.

After they went their separate ways to get to their places, the three of us were about as giddy and even more excited for the wedding as we possibly could be. Carder and I thanked Jude for bringing us to such a special moment and followed the bride and groom's previous actions; it was almost show time.

Upon returning to where the ceremony was taking place, it was pretty packed. But beautiful to think that all of us are here to witness these two awesomely in love people be united.

Carder and I took our seats with cute bulletins waiting to be opened; we quietly sat next to some of Angelo's relatives. Shortly after that, the wedding began.

To signify the beginning of the wedding, the wedding march song thing typically begins to play. Of course, this is not a typical couple or ceremony.

A soft, familiar tune began playing over the speakers around the garden. It was a beautiful tune being played on the piano, but I couldn't place what song it was. I was about to lean in and quietly asked Carder if he knew, but before that could even go into action, he pointed to a page he had opened in the bulletin that had the name of the song listed.

A slowed-down piano version of the song '*I'm Gonna Be (500) Miles*' originally sung by *The Proclaimers* but covered by *Sleeping at Last*.

This was just sort of absolutely perfect.

Julia had Bridesmaids holding small bouquets of flowers along the outside of the isles, but her, dare I say, lovely Maid of Honor came gracefully strolling down with Angelo's best man Lucca.

Jude and Lucca were good sports about it. They were silly but completely formal at the same time; both hooked at the arm because you gotta keep it traditional in some aspect, right?

Jude's pocket square was the color and material of the Bride's Maids dresses; this was probably the most adorable thing I have ever seen.

The garden was full of giddiness as Jude and Lucca met Angelo at the end of the aisle. But that was hushed away as Julia rounded the corner and began her first steps down the beautiful path, her parents on each side.

This feeling swept through me as she walked past us like I was watching a movie being made or I had front-row seats to this outstanding play. Carder and I held hands, trying to compress the excitement in our palms.

Isn't this crazy?

No,

It is crazy.

Carder and I have known Jude for a brief amount of time.

Half that time, we didn't even know his real name!

And here we are.

We've only met Julia once;

Under horrible circumstances,

And here we are.

But here, where we are, I couldn't feel more-

I can't even find a word for it,

I can't really use Fancy-dancy©,

That's improper use of such a great word.

I was gently nudged out of my thoughts before I could find a replacement word, and in perfect timing, too, Julia had just reached Angelo. Carder knows when I'm up in Lucy Land and need to return.

I swear everyone lost it inside as Julia and Angelo reached for each other's hands. I was hearing sniffling like nobody's business.

I'm not complaining because I was very much contributing to that.

I noticed something, though,

Something was missing,

And it's a pretty important piece of a wedding ceremony;

The Officiant.

Where in the heck was the-

Lo and behold, the Universe read my mind.

Coming up from around the garden came Amadore, dressed to the nines in quite the Officiant get-up.

He smiled at the crowd, who got a bit of comic relief that he was the one officiating the wedding. He began the ceremony with a prayer in Italian; the translation was in the cute little bulletin.

Might I just say that Italian is such a gorgeous language?

Alright, now back to the beautiful people getting married.

I swear there wasn't a dry eye in this garden; I can't see Mr. Johnson's face that well, but I bet my slice of cake that his tear ducts are ready to go.

Who am I kidding, though.

My 'slice' of cake.

I am most certainly having more than one piece.

And as ridiculous as Amadore was last night, he really did a terrific job. I'm sure that didn't just surprise me. When the magic words came off his lips after saying the age-old proclamation in Italian and English, everyone stood up and cheered, clapped, and cried!

Two odd young adults may have made complete fan-girl noises as the bride and groom shared their first kiss as a married couple and became the De'Amores. Who could blame those dorks!

It was such an incredible, sensational experience; everyone was just so happy for these two people, who were sharing a kiss that I dare say comes pretty darn close to the kiss *Wesley and Buttercup* share at the end *of Princess Bride.* I don't take that reference lightly.

It was like time had slowed down, just for us to enjoy these pure moments of complete happiness with no regrets or worry about the future; it was beautiful.

I turned to Carder, who was clapping and crying tears of joy, and as he turned to me, this was a new Carder face.

He looked so still. Everything behind him was moving and jumping for joy; people were throwing confetti in the air they brought with them, and here he was, looking back at me with his eyes filled with this stillness and a smile that captured the very feeling I was trying to describe in my mind.

Everyone looked at Julia and Angelo, the power couple of the year.

Everyone was expecting their kiss, obviously.

But I wasn't expecting the feeling I felt a moment later as the cheering and whistling went on; the confetti still flew, and lives were being changed forever.

Carder had kissed me.

10. The Business of Memories 

What.

In the heck,

Was *that?*

The question kept circling over and over. Rinse and repeat, around my mind, through all the slips and cracks of stupid and farfetched scenarios.

Was it really *that* farfetched, though?

Given the fact that Carder just decided to kiss me.

Me.

The person who refers to my entire wardrobe as '*Borderline Publicly Decent*' planted one right on me with what looked like zero hesitation.

Has he, like, thought about doing this before?

He has gotten into the shower with me, technically twice.

Held me at my lowest.

No, this just wasn't adding up.

Or,

Am I just overthinking this whole thing, and the kiss was induced by the excitement of young but true love?

So, he thought: *'Hey! I want me some of that!'*

Looked to the closest, most familiar person, and bam! It was lucky ol me.

To be frank, I have no idea which of these scenarios I would choose to be accurate; I'd much rather just be hit on the head, forget the last few minutes, and call it a day. Too bad I don't have a disorderly, happy-go-lucky batter on speed dial to help me out.

Goodness, what has this world come to?

While all these thoughts kept dancing around my head, I watched the guests and family members dance like there was no tomorrow in the Johnson's ballroom. Which was known to be called *'The middle room'* and most recently changed to *'The Illuminating Ballroom.'*

What a snappy name, indeed.

And gosh, did they really go all out; this place looked directly from a Pinterest pin on someone's dream wedding board. I know for sure it would be on mine.

Hanging lights above, but at just the proper exposure, you could see the natural light still coming from the vast glass ceiling.

I couldn't wait to eat the food; there was a huge buffet.

And I didn't forget about the cake;

But of course,

Lucy never forgets about cake.

There was an open bar which, I'm sure, will produce quite the stories by tomorrow morning; this place was very much in the business of making memories.

I was sitting at a nicely decorated table after joining everyone in, watching the newlyweds break a beautiful glass vase on the ground.

No, they weren't violently throwing glass, and the rest of us were cheering for more broken glass. I learned from Amadore that breaking a vase is a fun and beautiful tradition in Italian culture.

When a vase shatters on the ground, most people will associate that with panic; alas, in this case (or shall I say in this vase), it's anything but that! It's exciting; there's an underline of adrenaline and a huge dash of romance. The broken pieces of the vase represent the years of happiness for the bride and groom.

And damn, was that vase destroyed.

As the lights from the DJ booth slowly spun amongst the walls, it gave my eyes something to look at besides staring at people who can actually dance. Curse those people who can cleverly move their feet in rhythmic movements without even blinking an eye. And here I am, struggling to walk and make a human connection if I feel like taking a risk.

After Carder returned from his trip to retrieve my phone from the room, which was nice of him to offer, I tried to forget about the kiss. Maybe he's doing the same?

And if not,

Well,

That's just how it's going to be right now. I'm too invested in this true love thing and cake desire to deal with his abrupt actions right now.

"One of Angelo's cousins told me they aren't IDing at the bar. I'm thinking of snagging some wine. Do you want a glass? Feeling a little classy tonight, Madam?"

I smiled; hopefully, it didn't come across as awkward as I waved the question away.

With a shrug, he dance-walked his swinging hips to the bar and got a thinly shaped glass of white wine.

I didn't want to be on my phone tonight.

I wanted to be totally captivated and taken in by this breathtaking scenery.

The wonderful company,

The jiving music,

And yes, but of course, the cake.

But before diving in, I wanted to check and see if my parents had texted me.

Maybe I'll be popular on the one night I don't want to be!

As it turns out,

Nope,

Not unless getting texts from your boss is the new popularity.

Popularity is overrated.

Bookman Alan: *Lucy*

Bookman Alan: *This is of urgency.*

Bookman Alan: *Reply to me.*

Goodness gracious Alan; well, hopefully, everything is okay. Maybe he just needs help making a decision on the remodeling. Course, I don't know why he'd text me with assistance in that department; that's all Carder.

Me: *Sorry! I had my phone put away for the ceremony, is everything okay?*

Quickly I put my phone down so I didn't receive an unwanted lecture from Mr. Soon-to-be-Tipsy.

Carder's not much of a drinker. In fact, the only time I've seen him drink besides communion is when we decided to take a sip of my parent's champagne on New Year's when we were in High School. It had a snap to it, and of course, we wanted to try another taste because we already felt 'wasted' from that tongue dip we claimed as a swig.

With that said, tonight shall definitely be interesting. I've decided to measure it in the amount of glasses Carder drinks.

Half a glass in:

Carder has made the table I'm sitting at his pit stop between songs to take another drink of his wine and two sips of the water that I grabbed him because I am not taking care of a sick Carder tonight.

He will stay hydrated on my watch.

His drunken ass will stay hydrated with class.

OoooOoooOo-

I like that rhyme.

Multiple people came up to me and asked: *'what's my boyfriend's name?'* throughout this time. After politely answering, *'Oh, he's not my boyfriend, his name is Carder,'* I dropped the awkward Oh and left it at *'His name is Carder'*.

And my goodness, has he stolen Julia numerous times from Angelo. I had to physically take him off the dance floor and sit next to me during their first couple dance. Lord have mercy, the events that would have unfurled if he had bumped Angelo out of the way during that dance. And we are still only half a glass into the night.

Angelo's family is a riot; I've never seen a group of people with such gracious knowledge of how to have a good time.

To them, it was so simple, so natural; do they know what an awkward silence is? Have they had the same agonizing regret latch onto their vocal cords at the thought of an icebreaker game? Would embarrassment or shame ever dare to step into the temple of their gorgeous figures and strong independent minds?

Of course not!

These are golden people.

These are the Kings and Queens,

Emperors and Empresses of partying.

I shall never forget this night.

I could and am learning a lot from his family, but to be perfectly honest, I'm afraid to go out there to dance like Carder is. Granted, he's had a few sips of a confidence boost, but still, even if he didn't have anything to drink, he'd be dancing up that dance floor anyway.

I want to dance; as stupid and pathetic as it may sound, I just don't know how. My body literally rejects rhythm.

Like a Carder to a camouflage pantsuit- rejected.

While I giggled at the image of Carder in a camouflage pantsuit, I was accompanied by none other than the flawless bride, Mrs. De'Amore. I was awestruck even with her sitting next to me; she was just so gosh darn breathtakingly beautiful in the simplest way. Don't ask me to explain it; you can't explain such things. They just are.

"Why hello there, newlywed!" I smiled and tried to talk over the music and cheering guests. "You look so beautiful; I'm so happy for you!"

She could make a meat lover smile at a vegan restaurant in the middle of a vegan rally on *Vegan Island*. I don't know why said meat lover, or Julia, would be there, but hey, look, they're both smiling!

"Oh, you're too kind, thank you, I'm delighted you guys made it! It wouldn't have been the same without you and that silly guy who,"

Both of our gazes drifted to the dance floor, where we saw Carder dancing to a romantic-sounding Italian song with Angelo.

"Who is currently dancing with my husband."

We both started laughing as we watched the two men dance, rather well, I should add, amongst the other couples.

Julia sighed softly, "I wish I could get Jude to dance with me."

As much as I didn't want to take my eyes off Carder and Angelo, they shifted directly to Julia. Whose eyes were focused on her hand resting on the table.

"I know and respect why he doesn't, usually. But, just for today, this one day, I want to dance with my brother."

Her fingers were tightly closed,

"At least,"

Almost like she was afraid if she opened her hand, all the feelings she was holding inside would slip out between her fingers.

"With one of my brothers."

I wanted to place my hand on top of hers and give her a comforting squeeze, like the reassurance squeeze Carder and I do, but my hand wouldn't move.

"Look at me, being a downer at my own wedding, isn't that sad," Julia's fingers released their tension.

And my head turned to her leaving my previous thoughts behind. I shook my head at her statement.

"I'm not sad though, don't worry, I'm going to go get my husband. Would you like to help me?"

There goes that smile again, getting me up and onto the dance floor; that damn Johnson smile is going to get me into trouble one of these days.

Approaching the dance floor, the romantic song had ended, and one of the all-time must-have wedding reception songs came on.

None other than the fabulous *Whitney Houston classic 'I Wanna Dance with Somebody.'*

This is everyone's jam; if it's not, you're lying to yourself.

Right when that first note jazzed its way out of the tall speaker Carder and I involuntarily locked eyes. Something took us over like this was not a course of willing action. We were being possessed by the ghost of 80's past. And I totally consent, and I do not need an exorcism.

Carder gracefully twirled away from Angelo, trying to keep his composure as his hands were welcomed by his wife. While my 'all so serious' wedding date was mixing disco with tango for a fun dance flavor: *D i s a n g o.*

His eye contact was so silly and direct it would have been uncomfortable if I hadn't known him for so many years. Before he placed his hand on my waist, he kicked up his leg with a pointed foot.

I loved this dramatic style, like a language, of dance. Carder was quite fluent, while I was trapped in this awkward language barrier.

Do I move my hips?

Can my hips even move?

Damn these hips; I have the hips of the father in *Footloose.*

But for tonight, these awkward hips are leaving their little non-rhythmic box and entering the colorful world of dance. Or at least try. With the help of Carder, I barely got by in the dancing, but I was having fun.

Me! I was actually having a lot of fun!

My smile was so wide my cheeks started to hurt a little; I looked at all the people around us in flashes of movement from Carder swinging me around. And during it all, I caught a glimpse of Jude sitting at a table watching.

He smiled; it seemed he was probably having a good time, but it made me sad to see him just sitting there.

After this song, I'm going to try and get him on this dance floor. It'll take a miracle, but I'm hoping there's some magic floating about in the air tonight.

Hell, there has to be! If I'm somehow dancing without tripping all over the place.

Just a few notes before the song had ended, I looked to the table where Jude had been, and it was empty. Turning to ask Carder if he had seen him, I found that Carder was finishing off the last of the wine in his glass.

Smirking from the sight, I turned toward the DJ booth, and there Jude was, looking all dapper.

He must have requested a song as he leaned toward the DJ. And as Jude returned to his personal bubble, his eyes shifted to mine.

Embarrassed, I looked away and then had to awkwardly move them back to his gaze to see he was laughing a little, which became contagious. I motioned him to come on over, and he was now leaning toward me in a moment so I could hear what he was saying.

"Are you enjoying your time in the *Illuminating Ballroom?*" His voice, I could tell, was pressing hard on his vocal cords, trying to be loud enough.

This attempt probably shouldn't have made me giggle, but hey, it's a giggly kind of night. "Why yes, I am sir, and you? You did wonderful in the ceremony!" I saw the creases of his smile and heard the soft exhale of his laugh.

Returning my eyes to the dance floor as he began to speak again because it somehow made it easier to hear amongst the chaos.

"Aw, why, thank you! That's very nice; Julia was absolutely stunning. I'm so happy for her!"

The excitement in his voice triggered me to look back at him again, but before my eyes moved, he added to his response.

"If I may be so bold, I think your night is about to get better."

Now that statement motioned my eyes to his; Jude had this calm glaze over them, this confidence that inspired me. I gave him a confused but happy expression, to which his response was a smile and the beginning notes of a song I hold dear to me.

'L-O-V-E' by Nat King Cole.

Wait-

As Jude smiled his mischievous grin, holding his arms out in a *look what I did* gesture, he made his way back to the table.

This sent my mind, my thoughts, back to a memory. A memory with him. A question he asked me on our first outing together. This song was playing in his jeep, and I got all giddy. "King fan, huh?" He asked me.

As I then proceeded to tell him if I could have any singer from the past sing at my wedding, it would be *Nat King Cole.*

I think Jude could tell I was processing the memory as I looked over at him; I shook my head with a wide uncontrollable smile as I walked over to him.

He had one of his legs over the other with his hands folded on his lap.

Standing next to him, hearing one another was a little easier. "You remembered,"

His response was a broader grin than before.

I put my hand out to him in the language of dance; its translation is *join me.*

To which his grin shrunk a little but not all the way.

Before it got awkward, a surprisingly fast two wine glasses in Carder swooped in and slipped his hand in mine.

"Lucy! You love this song! Let's put our swing dance lesson to good use!"

And away we went as I turned my head while being dragged out to the dance floor again. Jude was laughing, but I could tell it wasn't like our laughing before. It was more genuine moments ago, and now I feel bad for my naive ambitions.

The emotion was gracefully tossed aside as Carder spun me, and my dress chased behind. We became the dancing couple everyone began to watch. At first, I was utterly terrified, but we got so into it, and the dancing evolved naturally. We danced through two more songs without even noticing.

We are now four glasses of wine and one shot in:

Carder is holding up pretty well. The boy can hold his alcohol, thank God.

Taking occasional breaks between dancing and talking with Jude, Angelo, Julia, and the other guests, our day and night were going perfectly. I hardly looked at my phone at all.

After another group picture, Carder and I were back dancing.

Carder was sporting a lot of jazz hands tonight, which made me very happy.

As for myself, I broke out my special move- the running man, a few times. So, you could say I got a little wild tonight.

The first couple of notes sounded familiar in the transition of a new song. People started to cheer and exclaim in excitement:

> *'This is our song!'*

> *'I love this song!'*

> *'This is my shit!'*

They raced to the dance floor, prepared to belt out every word, as I was still trying to figure out what classic hit was playing.

And as the guitar riff came to an end,

it clicked,

and my body,

my mind,

everything froze.

I found myself politely making my way through the crowd of dancing and singing people; I could feel sweat beginning to make its way through my pores. I walked out of the ballroom. I could hear the music still, the song that flooded too many memories.

'Under Pressure,' by Queen and David Bowie.

I collapsed in a sitting position in a back hallway; it was dim, and the bit of light that barely reached me was coming from the ballroom. I held my hand to my chest. My heart was racing; I needed to calm down. I didn't want to have an attack right now, but as the thought crossed my mind, the pain signals in my brain were already sent out and at work. Why did this have to happen today of all days?

And if I wasn't stirred up enough, I was startled as footsteps echoed toward me, and a pair of knees fell to my side.

Jude's eyes were a mixture of confusion and fear.

We had matching eyes.

"I saw you leave," He gently pressed the back of his hand to my forehead. "Lucy, are you okay?" As he quickly examined my face, I guess I looked more pale than usual.

I know; how is that possible.

My hands were freezing as Jude held them in an attempt to warm them up. "Lucy, can I get you something? Do you need to go in? What-"

Another pair of knees appeared on my other side; Carder knew what was happening.

"Oh, Dear, come here, come here, it's okay." Carder wrapped his arms around me as my hands slipped out of Jude's.

"Carder, what's happening? What can I do? Please, I'm worried," Jude spoke quickly but clearly.

Carder didn't respond.

And I couldn't even begin to will my body to move or my mind to speak.

"Carder, please-"

"Oh my gosh, Jude, stop! You can't do anything to help; you don't under-stand what's happening; just leave, go back to the party!" He sounded so *mean*, with this tiny hint of concern that I think only I could hear because I knew Carder wasn't *trying* to be mean.

But to Jude, he probably just came off as a jerk. And it was a jerk move; he was only trying to help.

I could hear Jude's footsteps walk back to the drowning lyrics that submerged me into the darkest place I've been to. My whole body trembled, I couldn't control it, and the only thing my mind was focused on was Colin.

Carder held me, while in my mind, I was holding Colin.

He held my head gently to his chest as I remembered the faint feeling of my fingers through Colin's hair that was wet from the rain; he was so cold. I feel so cold.

I miss his brown hair.

His laugh.

The way he attempted to skip rocks.

And above all, his presence in my life.

At the beginning of the evening, I thought I would end up taking care of a drunken Carder. Well, surprise, surprise; here I am helpless and, in the hands, literally of a wine-filled Carder. I guess alcohol brings out this motherly side of him as he rocked me slowly, and with one of his hands, he rubbed my arm.

I was right about one thing, despite this occurring, I would never forget tonight.

After some time, I felt more at ease as I felt a vibration coming from Carder's pocket. We both readjusted as he reached in and took out my phone. He must have grabbed it off our table on his way out of the ballroom.

As he handed it to me, I thought of Jude and how he must be feeling. I feel so bad, so guilty.

I hope he and Carder make up, which I'm sure they will, or this will be an awkward car ride.

Unlocking my phone, I had 5 missed calls and 1 new text message from Alan.

Bookman Alan: *Things are not okay. Maybell and I are at the ER. Tom fell.*

11. Messy Balance

I could hear Carder ask me what was wrong, but I couldn't process, let alone release the right words to say in response. I felt my phone slip out of my hand and into Carder's, and shortly after, our troubled emotions mended together.

Carder's eyes pierced me with questions he wouldn't ask until one pushed itself through. "How are we going to tell Jude?" His voice sounded flat, but I knew better. He was scared but wanted to keep calm for *'my sake.'*

Poor Jude,

I have no idea how to tell him,

Or even when to bring it up,

It's his sister's wedding reception, for goodness sake!

There isn't a good time.

There's never a good time for such misfortunes.

"Well," staring at my feet like they would give me answers, "We can't just keep it from him. We have to tell him."

"I know we have to tell him; I just don't know when we should." Fumbling with his phone, he continued, "Plus, he probably thinks I'm a dick right now from yelling at him; damn, I suck. Look, I'm going to call Alan. Do you feel okay enough to go back and find Jude? Don't tell him quite yet; just see if he's okay, please?"

I nodded; it probably was best if I was the one to go find him. I'm sure he and Carder will be fine; the bromance shall prevail.

I knew probably only Jude noticed that I left the *Illuminating Ballroom*. However, I still felt self-conscious about entering all over again. I felt guilty walking into a room full of people laughing and making memories while I had this scary news tied to my still-recovering anxiety-riddled chest.

I shouldn't, but I do.

It's not my fault, but my mind is twisting it like it is.

I'm carrying around this awful news through this beautiful scene; I know it's said many times not to blame the deliver, but do we ever really listen to that?

I found Jude's eyes; they were looking at me with a hint of surprise that I was out and about. But as my gaze drifted down just a tad to see his goony smile, I felt a little balance in this messy mind of mine.

"And there she is!" He leaned into me a little, so I could hear him over the music. "Are you feeling okay? Would you like some water?"

I softly giggled at his kindness. "I'm okay, thank you though, I'll be okay. I'm sorry, I didn't mean to make a scene or something-"

Jude silenced me with the brush of his hand against mine, and it took everything in me not to look down and witness it. "You have nothing to be sorry about. The only thing you need to worry about is having a good time."

And damn it, that distracting smile got me once again; once again, for a moment, he made me forget everything. How can a human have that much power, not even realize it, and just have this adorable smile cover it all? How I wish that were the only thing, I needed to worry about. "Jude, are you okay? Carder didn't mean to yell at you. He just gets a little protective sometimes, I think."

He waved it off. "Oh, I know, I know, Carder and I are Pals. We're cool." This dork did a shaka sign with not one but both hands. How does he constantly make himself more and more adorkable?

Wait- Lucy,

Get back on track,

Stop admiring his hand moves,

There must be a better word for that,

UGH STOP- focus;

Tom.

I wonder if Carder has heard anything from Alan-

Speak of the devil; there Carder is, dancing his way towards us.

I feared it would be an awkward exchange when he finally got over to us. But instead, Carder and Jude did a bro hug like it was nothing, and the universe, well, most of it, was back on track.

I'll never understand guys.

But they're okay, so my comprehension of the male species doesn't matter right now.

Carder looked at me, and I knew what he was thinking; now may not be the best time, but we have to before we run out of time.

Dramatic but accurate.

How could I look at Jude's mile and reflect on it when I know I will break it within time?

I suppose we're all breakers of smiles at some point.

I wasn't quite ready for battle.

We mingled for a bit amongst the music and laughter until Jude wandered over to his sister and his new brother-in-law. Carder and I walked over to our table and sat down; he started drinking some water.

We shall miss wine Carder, but sober Carder is pretty grand as well.

"Carder, when are we going to tell Jude?" As he gulped down a second glass, I could tell he drank too fast because the icy water made his eyes squint.

He took a deep breath. "Well, they've finished doing all the important sentimental moments; I guess the next time he comes over here, we'll ask for a little meeting in the hallway?"

After about three more songs, Jude made his way over to us.

Glancing at Carder, he gave me a weak smile, then turned his eyes to Jude and put on a more reassuring smile. I looked around to take it all in before this next moment because, after this moment, the feeling won't be the same. I felt selfish for even thinking that.

And I believe Jude could see through Carder's smile as he exchanged glances with both of us, and Carder pitched him the hallway meeting idea.

12. Confuder©

Immediately after we delivered the news, Jude blankly reached for his phone. He calmly walked around the corner to place a call. Once he was out of our view, Carder and I turned toward one another in wonder and confusion; wonusion.

Or confuder.

I kind of like confuder better.

Another word for the Lucy Dictionary.

Confuder©.

Maybe he's trying to stay calm or so overwhelmed that his body is forcing him to be calm. Or that just happens to me because we all know Lucy's body *loves* to throw around irony and arbitrary.

I feel like Carder, and I both had the thought to go follow and check on him, but we stayed put and patiently waited for the plot twist to settle so we could all figure out our next step.

After about 10 minutes, Jude came walking back, and you could just feel the shift in his mood–obviously.

He told us that Tom was admitted to the hospital; Alan and Maybell brought him there after they found him on the ground by his porch when they went to check on him. So far, they didn't know how long he had been laying there; thank God they arrived when they did.

"I was hoping we'd be able to stay around New York for at least a day after the wedding so I could spend some time with my family," Jude said in a distant-sounding voice as his eyes were concentrated on the floor. "But I'm the only family Tom has, and he needs me. He really banged himself up on that fall; we'll have to leave in the morning." Jude's eyes caught me off guard as they shot up to me, almost like they were looking for a sign of clarity.

But sadly, I had none to offer; I was just as lost.

Carder quietly cleared his throat. "Is there anything we can do?" Sometimes it sucks throwing that question out there when you know there's no use for it, like throwing a fishing net into a decorative pond.

But of course, in all of Jude's composed politeness, he shook his head and told us it was still Julia's beautiful day. "Tom is stable, and if we left now, I don't know how much use we would be anyway because he probably needs to sleep. So, to the best of our ability, we should continue celebrating Julia and Angelo's awesomeness."

And once again, our small committee agreed as we made our way back to the reception.

Jude walked back into the *Illuminating Ballroom* like an actor swaggering back onto the stage with a painted face. Knowing he just had a tension-filled time backstage, the audience has no knowledge of this. The audience sees what you display and reacts to it.

And at this moment, it made me wonder how many performances we all must put on in our lifetime for the people around us, especially Jude. Cause goodness, watching him cross that threshold, I saw the sparked talent of an actor, or perhaps it's just an abundance of love for his dear sister. In any case, I couldn't help but wonder what was going on in his mind and how I could help. I suppose all I can do is what he asked until directed otherwise. So tonight, we shall dance amongst hidden terrible news. Or at least two of us will dance, and one will mingle and request songs.

As obedient committee members, we stayed true to our agreement. We would celebrate Julia and Angelo. Why Lucy even took an offered glass of wine from Carder.

Oh goodness,

and apparently, Lucy is a lightweight,

and intoxicated Lucy likes to talk in the third person.

Lucy will be switching to water, most likely after this glass. But during this glass, Carder and Lucy became the life of the dancefloor alongside Julia, Angelo, all the cousins, and some other wedding guests that they've become best friends with for the night.

During the laughter and grade-A dancing, Lucy looked over to see if she could spot Jude watching and laughing as well but instead, Lucy saw him talking with a couple. Something about their demeanor and Jude somehow sensing Lucy was looking at him and waving Carder, and Lucy over told Lucy they were important people. Intoxicated Lucy has some other heightened skills besides narration. She took Carder by the arm and began walking toward them.

"Hey, party animals!" Jude spoke loudly but with an air of sophistication.

Or Lucy is just perceiving things all silly like.

Jude gave a gentle smile. "They've been wondering who I'm spending all my time with nowadays."

Carder and Lucy quickly glanced at one another and put their *'proper-totally not tipsy-smiles'* on.

"Mom, Dad, this is Carder and Lucy."

They've now met the parents, Mr. and Mrs. Johnson; Carder and Lucy gave one another little smirks of relief at how *professionally* they handled that introduction.

Mrs. Johnson cleared her throat and smiled. "It really is so nice to meet you two, and what loyal friends you must be to travel all this way for such an exceptional occasion."

Okay, maybe Lucy is just mesmerized, but she is like if *Mary Poppins* and *Judge Judy* raised a daughter together, and Lucy is all for it.

Mrs. *Judge Poppins* continued, "We've lived an interesting life that always called for traveling. So, the kids never got to make solid friendships with people outside our little circle. And when Jude left for Virginia and made the sudden spontaneous decision to stay, well, we can't say we weren't concerned with wonder. But now I see, it's rare to come across such gems." She looked at her son and gently touched his face with a shine in her eyes. "But he better remembers his Mother and call if he's not going to visit as often." And there's *Judge Judy*; Mrs. Johnson needs to give Lucy life lessons.

Apparently, Lucy was zoning out, for Mr. Johnson went dancing with Julia, and Carder whisked Mrs. Johnson away on the dancefloor.

Now it was just the two of them, and Jude gave Lucy a little nudge. "How's the wine?" Giving her a grin as Lucy looked at him with a matching one. "Sorry my Dad didn't really say anything, but I can tell when he doesn't like people just by his body language, and don't worry, he likes you guys. I think he's just frustrated with me or something."

That caught Lucy a little off guard as Jude looked at his feet, and the lights of the DJ booth decorated the floor. Perhaps his Dad was upset that Jude wouldn't set aside his refusal to dance just this one day for his sister, or he's still bitter about Jude not coming back to New York. Should Lucy ask Jude if he's doing okay with the news of Tom?

"But,"

Nope, Lucy was too late.

"Anywho,"

No points for Lucy.

"Would you like some more wine, *Mrs. Cumberbatch*?"

Lucy hadn't heard that in a while; it made her blush. But Lucy politely shook her head and requested they get some water instead. There was too much third-person inner dialogue going on. She needed to sober up.

Jude found a table with a good view of the dancefloor nonsense, and like the gentlemen he is, he got a glass of water, a coffee for himself, and a bowl of pretzels. Him and his coffee pretzels. What a character.

After drinking about a cup of water, I could feel the tipsiness drifting away.

Bye-bye, tipsy Lucy.

You were a strange delight.

I have to say, Jude was taking this all very well; he genuinely looked to be having a good time. I knew how much he cared for Tom and how much Tom loved Jude. I just can't imagine Jude not being anxious right now. And a part of me really wants to ask him if he's okay, but I don't want to ruin whatever process he has going on that's holding him together.

I suppose if he wants to talk, he knows he can talk to me. But instead, we just laughed at the dancing and sang along to songs we knew. I got roped into dancing with Carder a few times and even some of Angelo's cousins. And while I was embraced by the music and groovy dancing, I would steal glances at that little table populated by the dork who made this all happen.

Jude would give me this smile as if I was dancing for the both of us. While I was dancing, his parents sat with him and talked. I wonder if he told them about Tom and our plans for tomorrow. When is the right time to deliver such news?

As the DJ announced that the last song for the night had been played, he called Angelo to come to speak on the mic per his secret request; I turned to see Julia's reaction, and she was surprised and puzzled.

Angelo stood on the DJ's platform and spoke with his fantastic voice into the mic. "Julia and I would like to thank everyone for coming; this has been the second-best day of my life."

You could see this adorable spark in his eyes, and you knew he was looking out to Julia like they were the only two in the room. Scratch that, the only two in the entire universe.

"The best day of my life was when I was just walking down the sidewalk, and I literally ran into this flustered American girl. The most beautiful human being I'd ever seen. Julia, my family, and I have been saving up for this special surprise. We're returning to our special moment- WE'RE GOING TO ITALY FOR OUR HONEYMOON!"

Everyone turned to Julia, crying joyfully while all the cousins cheered. Perhaps they planned this, but I wouldn't be surprised if it was spontaneous. They rushed to the DJ platform, and Angelo turned his back and fell backward as his cousins caught him. Angelo proceeded to body surf all the way to Julia. After they put him down and now the whole ballroom was cheering and chanting 'Kiss Kiss Kiss!' Julia and Angelo shared the most beautiful kiss I've witnessed since their romantic declaration earlier.

The giddy couple went to the main doors where they could individually thank and say goodbye to everyone. Amongst the line of continued celebrators and relatives, Carder and I heard the whispers that they were leaving first thing in the morning.

"I guess that may help Jude not feel so guilty about leaving for home in the morning," Carder said. As the word home came off his lips, I wondered if Jude considered Virginia Beach home.

Carder and I got to chat with the Johnson's a little while waiting, and it was confirmed that the happy couple was indeed leaving for Italy in the morning. Goodness, how exciting it would be to be in their shoes, how giddily amazing.

And speaking of giddy,

my date for the wedding-

was he my date?

I mean, together we

Drank,

Danced,

Had like two emotional episodes,

We got ready together,

He kissed me-

Goodness, gracious, maybe date doesn't even cover it. We sounded more like spouses doused in spontaneity for the day.

In any case, Carder had a very giddy glimmer in his eyes as we saw people leaving the residence for the evening because the party was over, but something told me Carder, and I had a second wave coming.

"Come on, come on, come on," Carder excitedly raddled off after we said our congratulations, goodbyes, and thank yous. He slipped his hand in mine and started pulling me out the doors of the Illuminating Ballroom.

Laughing while Carder dragged me along, I searched for those grey-blue eyes to signal that we were leaving to, well, who knows where. Just as we were about to cross the ballroom threshold, my eyes caught Jude's. He was talking with some of Angelo's cousins. He saw Carder dragging me like a five-year-old at a Zoo wanting to see the next exhibit and gave me a small chuckle as he disappeared from my view.

"Lucy, why do I feel like I'm dragging you- you should be excited; I'm a riot," We continued, now in a fast-paced walk, to the main entrance of the humongous gorgeous house.

"I don't know what wine Carder has up his sleeve; you can't blame me for being hesitant. I hardly know what to expect from sober Carder."

As he opened the doors to go outside and pulled us out there, in one swift-ass movement, he let go of my hand, picked me up bridal-style, and looked at me with wild, silly eyes. "Good! Just the way it should be!" Carder began spinning us in a circle as I naturally clutched tighter to him. He said in his sing-song way, "I'm crraaaazzzyyyyyy!"

I couldn't help but laugh and be slightly impressed he was not making himself sick from spinning.

Luckily, he stopped before any sickness was induced from either of us. We are not the spinning type. "And I'll be damned my Lucy-Lou has a boring life." Carder, catching his breath, smiled at me so widely.

"Then what do you suppose we do?" I felt a little self-conscious that he was still carrying me because I didn't know how heavy I felt, but then again, I didn't because it was Carder. He just made me laugh.

Once again, he smiled at me like he knew what I was going to say, and he already had a plan in motion. "The way I see it," He switched to a proper tone, silly still, of course, and walked while still carrying me down the front steps. "We have two options to continue this night with memories before we face tomorrow. I will be content with either because I am an amazing planner, so the choice is yours. First, please choose: inside or outside."

I should note two things:

1. Wine Carder is even more confident and sassy than Sober Carder, and this is a whole new pandora's box of opportunity.

2. While he was explaining this to me, he was dipping me up and down and side to side, still carrying me- like, has he been working out in secret or something?

I thought for a moment, and the chilly air confirmed my decision. "Let's go inside; I'm getting kind of cold."

As soon as he heard the word inside, he started running to our room with me in his arms. Carder put me down like halfway there, and then we raced.

And I won the race. It may be due to the fact that Carder was winded, but I'm still taking the victory.

Victory points for Lucy.

Once we made it to our room, I was ready to be *instructed* for this night of endless fun. And instructed I was.

Carder told me we should first change into comfy clothes, for it would be a cozy night.

I can't say I wasn't excited about this; fancy clothes are nice, but what a wave of enjoyment when you take them off and slip on sweatpants.

After we were all comfy in our attire, we sat down on the bed with a sigh of relief.

Carder laid on his back as I followed his lead. "Goodness, what a crazy-emotional-lovely-sad day. How are we supposed to feel right now?" He asked in a slightly joking/dramatic tone.

"I believe" I put my hands out like I was giving a motivational speech to the thousands in the audience just waiting to be inspired. "We have the right to feel tired."

"And tipsy"

"You're still tipsy?" I laughed in disbelief, well, sort of disbelieve.

"Gurl, I was following orders; it was a day of celebration."

"Speaking of which, might I ask what your plan was for our furthered night of celebration?"

And with that simple question, of course, came an extravagant response from our extravagant Carder. He jumped up to his knees and leaned his head over mine with a whimsical glimmer in his eye. "I thought it would be most appropriate to build a fort,"

I gave him a pondering smile.

He read my mind's question, "I remember your family used to have fort days, and they were especially fitting when you had a rough day. And though this day was filled with a lot of happiness, it also had some rough moments. So, I thought, what better way to end the day than in a fort where we can hide away from the rough parts and fill it with happiness."

By the end of his sentence, I was smiling so big I sat up and launched a big hug to him immediately. "That sounds like the most delightful idea Carder, thank you," Releasing him and reflecting on his smile.

We sat up with a new playful tone filling the room as we played some upbeat 80s ballads and began creating our magical fort. Man, it's been forever since I've made a fort.

We took the sheets and blankets off the beds and pulled the sheet over the gap between the two beds creating a comfy crawl space underneath. Then we weighted the sheet down on both sides so it wouldn't fall, and we piled the pillows and blankets we had for a maximum comfort fort. Even the lamp came down by us so we could shut off the ceiling light in the room to give the experience a calmer tone.

And just to further illustrate how extra we are: giggly, we snuck out of our room to the cottage's kitchen, and we found scissors, paper, and a pen. We returned to our room, and Carder drew individual stars on the paper. At the same time, I cut them out and then set them on top of the thin sheet so we could look at our makeshift solar system while lying down in our fort.

My goodness, we are as cool as it gets.

Once the final star was cut and placed, we crawled under our new night sky and laid on our backs; surprisingly and satisfyingly comfortable, this fort is.

I looked at Carder from the corner of my eye and saw how big his smile was as mine grew to match it. "This is so awesome. You were right; this is a great night of continued memories." Still looking at him, he turned his head to me. "Thank you, Carder. You've always had a knack for making life interesting."

Although seeing his smile grow only brought more joy to mine, I was speaking the absolute truth. Throughout our entire friendship, even the way we became best friends, Carder has always made things fascinating and fabulous in the best possible way.

"Well, you, LucyLou, have always been there for me. And though I love myself, I also know I am not always glamorous to be around."

I gave him a slightly playful glare.

"Seriously though, I don't know what I would do without you. My life has been an adventure since I met you." His smile was still present, but it had a touch of fragileness to it now, and as I was about to say something and as I felt Carder's hand brush against mine, there was an unexpected knock at the door.

I looked at him in confusion and kind of smiley at the oddness of it; he looked to me a little flustered but not to the point where he was trying to show it. What is going on with him?

Carder crawled from the fort to the door as I got on my stomach and poked my head out of the blanketed oasis to see who our possible late-night guest was. And to our pleasant surprise, it was a dapper strawberry blonde gentleman in cozy PJs.

"Hey late nighters, I hope I'm not intruding," Jude greeted us with a smile and kind of a nervous posture. "I can't really fall asleep, and I can't deny that I'm not worried about Tom" He took a short pause to glance at his feet.

I took a moment to look at Carder, but he didn't look at me.

"And you guys are like my best friends, so I was just wondering if maybe I could crash with you guys for the night. I'll sleep on the floor; that's totally fine."

"Aren't you in luck" I chimed in, trying to lighten the heaviness of the room. "We're already sleeping on the floor!" I made as grand of a gesture as I could, still lying on my stomach and my head only partially out of the fort.

Jude smiled at me and checked to see Carder's reaction, to which Carder was already walking away from the open door. Not much of a warm welcome. I can't see why Carder would be annoyed; we all get along pretty well?

I waved for Jude to come into the room, and as he shut the door, Carder crawled under the fort and laid on his back on the one side of me; I repositioned myself to also be on my back. Looks like I'll be sleeping in the middle. In the short seconds I had before Jude would enter the fort, I nudged Carder and mouthed, *'What's wrong?'*

He quickly whispered, *"I wanted to have that special moment; it was like my Oscar-winning moment."*

Which prompted me to whisper back, *"You're dramatic; I'm sure you'll have many more of those in your life."*

And then he whispered, *"The scene is ruined."*

Jude crawled his way, gracefully, into the fort.

I looked to Carder to try to read his face, but he gave me no indication of how he felt. Which made it all the more strange.

"Guys, this is amazing! I love the stars," Jude complimented us as he nestled in, laying on his back.

That may be the only comfortable way to sleep tonight, at least for the two of us; Carder has already turned on his side with his back facing me.

Jude and I pretended to point out constellations and reminisced some fun moments we had today. I wanted to try to help distract him from his worries about Tom. I was worried for both of them, especially with the lingering words Tom left me with one of the last times we talked.

'I can tell, I can tell I'm gonna be checkin' out soon.

I had to tell someone; I can't tell JudieBoy.'

I almost felt guilty holding this information, not that it was a set-in-stone fact. Tom just said he had a feeling. But maybe I should have told Jude by now; if it were me, would I have wanted him to?

But as we lay there and I felt the small amount of sheltered heat mingling between my arm and Jude's. And the absence of Carder's giddiness, I felt a tightness in my throat like I couldn't say anything. This moment seemed like the last of somewhat normalcy; after tomorrow, we didn't really know what would happen.

Tomorrow was the door to uncertainty; at least we're all walking in together.

13. To The Surface 

The morning sun was not shy in waking us up, nor was Carder's alarm. Though one could argue that waking up to the bubbly New York City sunlight and the always incredible voice of *Barbra Streisand* wasn't the worst way to start a day. I could have hit that snooze button a dozen times.

We were going to be driving back to the formally ordinary life of Virginia Beach; truthfully, we didn't know what would unravel once we got there.

Jude excused himself from the room after we all got our grumpy morning moans out, so he could pack up and get ready. Before he left, we all agreed to meet in the front by the musical Jeep in about an hour. While Jude left, he received a phone call from Alan; I hope it was an update of some good news.

As the door shut, I turned to Carder and gave him a slanted expression. "I feel so bad," Speaking my concerns into existence as I helped Carder take down our little one-night paper-star haven. "I really hope Tom is okay."

Carder got most of the fort down already. "I hope so too. I'm glad Alan was there."

My head subconsciously jerked up at him.

"I know; I never thought I would say a sentence like that either."

We both laughed a little, which didn't entirely feel right, but it felt right to share a laugh with him. I cleared my throat a little "Do you think the car ride back is going to be okay?"

With a bit of confusion and preoccupied with bedsheets, Carder replied, "Why wouldn't it be Lucy-Lou?"

It usually makes me grin when he says that, but this time I shrugged. "I don't know. I'm just worried the car ride may be weird or feel high-strung because of everything going on."

"Well, rest assured, your Majesty," he graciously pointed to himself, "I'll handle any awkwardness or tension that may occur. I checked the weather; it's going to be hot. I'd wear the jean shorts that I packed for you." Giving me a wink, and then he went off to get ready.

Such dramatic royalty he is, but I will take his suggestion; I don't want to be a sweaty mess in the Jeep.

Just as he said, the jean shorts were waiting for me, and as I grabbed them, I contemplated if I should double-check if my legs needed to be shaved or not. That seemed like way too much effort for a long ass car ride. So, on the shorts went along with a comfy t-shirt and my trusty converse. And my hair is just going to rock a very lazy ponytail today.

I waited on the bed with my bag packed up, waiting for Carder.

He really went hard for this road trip: He showered and shaved his face, wearing some very nice shorts with a matching shirt, and his hair was so nicely sculpted.

And then there was me, with all my comfy effort, and what I thought was radiant judgment from Carder turned into his classic kiss on the forehead.

Which I love receiving, but I thought for sure I was going to be roasted.

"Ready to go, hot stuff?"

I couldn't help but geek out in disbelief, but I was not in the mood to acknowledge his lack of acknowledgment of my lack of fashionable effort.

As we made our way outside, we saw Jude and his family saying their pleasant goodbyes. He and Julia made a running start to hug one another, and it was the purest thing. It was adorable to see what a profound and fantastic sibling relationship they have. It reminded me of Coli-

"Carder! Lucy!" Julia saw us and joyfully shouted for our attention, "Come say goodbye to your new family members!"

I think Carder and I just briefly died of wholesomeness. We glanced at each other with glossy eyes and then ran to our new little family.

When I say ran,

I mean, we walked over there in a timely manner.

Let's not get carried away here.

We don't do cardio.

We both shook Mr. and Mrs. Johnson's hands and thanked them for letting us stay in their beyond remarkable home. Geez, I still can't believe this is their home like they come here to recoup, and everything this is theirs.

Mind-blowing.

We gave Julia and Angelo, the adorable newlyweds, a hug goodbye and wished them the best of travels for their honeymoon. I'm so happy for both of them. They just genuinely seem to be the best fit for one another.

As I hugged Julia, Carder was talking with Angelo, and Jude was talking with his parents. Amongst their preoccupied moments, Julia and I had one of our own.

"Please look out for Jude," Julia whispered in her calm and nurturing voice. Ironically both broke and tenderized the innocent little goodbye hug we were having as we were still hugging. "I don't mean that you have to take care of him. He can take care of himself, but if you could just check in on him emotionally," she paused, "He'll never say out loud that he needs that or burden anyone with it. Still, I can tell you and Carder mean a lot to him, and he'd probably just appreciate that from you." Julia moved, so we weren't really hugging anymore, and she was looking at me now with a less severe face and a playful smile. "Jude can be pretty silly. But underneath that quirkiness is a soul that needs some checking in on every once in a while."

I gave her a reassuring smile and a nod. "Of course, Jude has been there for me, and I'll be there for him. I know Carder will, too; we've all grown pretty close in a short time."

Julia and I closed off our moment with a shared smile as we joined our attention back with the group.

I think Jude told his family the news about Tom sometime this morning or last night because we caught just the very end of his conversation with his parents. Reminding him to keep them updated and if there's anything they can do to let them know. It was nice to see that caring side of them.

And after the little chat, I just had with Julia, I can't lie; when I looked over at Jude, I felt worried about him all over again. And as we put our bags in the musical Jeep, I just kept hoping everything would be okay.

Carder can tell when I get anxious; he nonchalantly slipped his hand into mine, gave it a squeeze, and quietly asked if I was okay, to which I gave him a nod he didn't believe.

Before I could ask if Carder wanted to sit in the front or back seat, he climbed in the back and got comfortable while I settled into the passenger seat. Jude was running into the glorious house, which I still can't believe was theirs, because he forgot his charger.

In our small wait, I was going to find a cassette to start our trip. As I reached to open the glove compartment and looked down, my self-conscious mind went into a panic. "Carder, Carder emergency,"

"What'd you do now," He said in an uninterested monotone. Still trying to be comfortable, like a dog doing circles on its bed. He'd kill me if he knew I used that analogy in my mind.

I rolled my eyes. "Knees," still in a panic.

"What?"

"Knees-"I turned myself around, facing him now with my dread-riddled eyes "HAIRY KNEES, I HAVE HAIRY KNEES."

Carder automatically matched my distraught tone. "LUCY, HOW DO YOU FORGET TO SHAVE YOUR DAMN KNEES? THEY'RE LITERALLY THE GLUE TO YOUR LEGS, WHICH" He paused and leaned over for a second to look at my legs. "Are very nice, by the way. Can we just take a minute to talk about them-"

"No! We don't have a minute!" My arms took on a flabbergasted life of their own.

"Okay, fine, but this will be discussed."

"FOCUS. What am I going to do? It's so noticeable, especially in the sun.

Oh my gosh, WHY DIDN'T YOU NOTICE?"

"Okay, first off," Sassy Carder, "I don't have a knee fetish, and secondly, if I didn't notice, I highly doubt anyone else will." Sassy Carder is turned off for now. "You're fine. You look good; you always do."

As I was about to question him again out of my worry about having hairy legs, my piling questions were halted as Jude opened the door and buckled in. Carder's probably right. I'm sure he won't notice, and who cares anyway.

Legs are legs, damn it.

Set the knees free-

The glue to your legs, that was funny.

It doesn't pain me so much this time to do this.

Props are given when deserved:

Point for Carder.

As the musical Jeep started to stroll, I began to think of things to talk about during our ride to pass the time and perhaps comfort Jude and get his mind off Tom. I know I couldn't take his mind completely off it, but I could try my best.

I waited until we got on the main highway to start a conversation, and it appeared Carder read my mind.

"So!" Carder clapped, apparently to signify his presence, but let's be honest, who could forget such a radiant human like that? "What was every-one's favorite part of being in NYC?"

That was a good question. I felt like I had to ponder it for a moment to

get a good answer. I snuck a peek at Jude to see if the question intrigued that delicate silly spark in his eyes; it was kind of there but not all the way.

"If it pleases the council, I have an answer right away unless someone would like to go first?" Jude spoke like we were in an official meeting room instead of a Jeep.

I believe no matter his mood, he'll always be a little dorky. Carder and I looked at each other, *'officially,'* and agreed that he could go first in sharing.

"Why, thank you, fellow members,"

My goodness, he makes me giggle.

"I think my favorite part was just being there with Julia on her big day, that really meant a lot to me, and I know it did for her too. And seeing my parents was nice. It's been a little while, and seeing you guys meet them was both entertaining and lovely to witness."

How does a fella go about using a word like lovely and expect me not to feel something towards him?

Do I feel something towards him?

I mean,

at this point,

who even knows what I feel or want?

I'm a hot mess.

With hairy knees.

"Julia looked so stunning, and her happiness just radiated. I'm so happy for her. Man, she really deserves this. What a badass she is. When they get back from their honeymoon, she'll be taking on more responsibility for our Dad's company; kind of like a gradual transition for her to take over and for him to retire. Thank God she has an interest in that."

I looked at him before his sentence ended, and as his last word was said, he glanced at me and dazzled me with a sweet grin. And there he was, back for I don't know how long, but my goodness, did it make me smile. "How about you, Miss Lucy, any favorite moments?"

Hearing him call me that again made me unconsciously smile a little too big as I transitioned into my thinking expression, "Hmm, that's so hard. There were so many little moments to appreciate." I looked out the window to sort through the newly cataloged memories. "The wedding itself was gorgeous. I feel like that's an automatic answer, so secondly, I would say meeting all of Angelo's cousins and hanging out with them the night before, and dancing at the wedding was a lot of fun." For some reason, after I said dancing, I felt kind of guilty.

"That party was wild, and I kicked ass at that ping-pong competition. But my favorite part was definitely the ceremony, especially the end, absolutely beautiful."

I wanted to turn around to see Carder's face. What did he mean by the end? When they kissed or when he spontaneously kissed me?

Geez, I actually like almost forgot about that. So much has been going on since that moment.

Is that why Carder has been acting weirdly because we haven't talked about it? But then again, he hasn't brought it up, and I didn't think it was completely serious, given that he didn't address it.

Sometimes in conversations, I'd say mostly when people are in the car, it can be really easy for the conversation to just abruptly end. But it doesn't feel as harsh because there's most likely music playing, and you can see the things passing you by. But after Carder said his favorite part, we sat in that orbited silence for quite some time.

I didn't really feel pressure to talk or anything. However, I did wish there was music playing and found it odd that Jude didn't request a cassette chosen at random. But we all were sort of lost in our own minds, I think. Maybe we were all pondering similar situations, along with ones of our own, and probably random thoughts mixed in.

I thought about Tom, hoping he was feeling okay emotionally and physically in the hospital. I could only imagine that he was thinking of his precious wife. I think I would be if I was in his shoes. By how Tom talks about her, she must always be twirling about his mind.

I thought about Carder kissing me and what that was supposed to mean. I'm caught between everything in life having meaning, or sometimes things just happen, and they aren't supposed to be looked into that much.

But shouldn't everything in life have meaning? Every detail complies to mean something, or would that make life too exhausting?

What would I want the kiss to mean anyway, other than just being confused at this point. If it does mean something, Carder will address it. I'll leave it at that for now.

Then I thought about Jude.

Every now and then, I would look over at him and quickly observe his facial expression before he realized I was looking at him. Sometimes he looked like he was just resting his face, other quick glances, he looked deep in thought, but mostly he looked lost.

It sucks when you see that expression on someone's face, and you care and want to guide them out, but sometimes that's not your job. Your job is to just be there. Hopefully, Jude knows that; I think he does, given Carder and I are on this trip with him.

Then randomly, thinking about being on this trip, I thought about what happened to Carder's car before we left.

The slashed tires,

Changing cars,

The strange evidence I found stuck in the tire.

I didn't even have time to process that when it first happened. It was so chaotic trying to get on the road, and then once we were, I was excited and nervous to leave Virginia Beach.

And now that we're heading back, it's back in my mind.

I found a playing card,

folded and shoved into the slash of the tire.

The back design was scraped off to reveal a rough white background.

Obviously not in the best shape.

It was the king of hearts.

Just like the one I saw on Jude's counter a while ago.

Putting that together made my stomach a little upset; what was that supposed to mean? It's way too random to just be something to glaze over. So really, how can details of our lives be ignored? These things don't just happen. There're no coincidences; Sherlock Holmes would be all over this.

But what does this have to do with the Sherlock sitting next to me?

I don't want to jump to conclusions or start acting weird around him, but there's a connection between him and the card.

Was that the same card or is it a different one?

But what benefit would Jude have in slashing Carder's tires,

hiding the card, and then taking his Jeep instead? That wouldn't make any sense.

But maybe he really thinks he is like Sherlock Holmes, and he's trying to create some weird case for us to solve because he's insane.

No.

No, he doesn't seem like the kind of person to do that.

Jude is odd,

but not that type of odd.

I don't even really know when or how to bring up the card or if I should.

Well, of course, I should, even if it meant that he'll know I was kind of snooping, and the card caught my eye.

Why do I feel all this pressure to keep it to myself?

Especially with what's going on with Tom and being worried about him and Jude-

But I suppose when is a good time to bring a weird-ass mystery to the surface?

14. Uncashed Memories 

When I thought about the ride back, I envisioned music, laughs, and reminiscing. Perhaps even stopping at some diner with an unusual theme and then swearing to each other that we'd make this annual tradition.

But the ride back had an itinerary of mostly silence and out loud questions of whether we should get off this next exit or not to use the restroom and or get snacks. Carder and I changed seats once, and then Jude and Carder traded off driving.

It was pretty quiet, but the radiance of all our racing thoughts almost felt like an undertone frequency in the car. It felt unnatural for the group of us to not have music playing in the car, which made me think of the times we've blasted music on a drive. With all of us together and on separate occasions with Carder and Jude. I wonder what kind of musical memories we could have created, the different songs we would have belted out, hearing our offkey voices. I suppose those will just have to be made another time. I'm sure they will; potential memories must be cashed in at some point. They can't just go to waste, or I surely hope they don't.

I was slightly disappointed at the comfort and relief I felt when I saw the welcome sign to Virginia Beach. I was hoping, after this trip, seeing that sign would give me more bravery-induced inspiration to travel and explore more. But I just felt the ease of finally echo in my brain.

Then again, I shouldn't be so hard on myself; we are in an emergency situation. Of course I'd want us to get here quickly.

Once we entered the city limits, we headed straight for the hospital to be with Tom. Jude looked a little tired; surprisingly, Carder didn't, as we made our way into the inhabitance of florescent lights, distant noises, and hushed tension. Tom must have had Jude down as an emergency contact or something, so he was allowed to go back and be with him.

I imagined Tom initially filling out that portion of his paperwork with 'Judieboy' for the name. For relation, he would just put 'Judieboy' again.

Like the last time we all found ourselves in a hospital, which was quite strange, Carder and I took up temporary residence in the waiting room area.

Tom was in the ICU, so the waiting room we were currently in was a little comfier, in a hospital-type way. It made me kind of sad to think; this waiting room is probably set up the way it is because people often have to stay here longer.

All the families, children, significant others, and siblings that have waited within the neutral walls of this room with the company of paintings that have close to no depth. Waiting in painful silence for some sort of update that, with passing time, seems the only possible result will be inevitably bad.

"Lucy," Carder tapped my hand, "Doing okay?" thank God he pulled me out of that messy summersault of thoughts I had going on that was getting darker than I cared for.

I moved my hand to momentarily hold his so I could give it a slight reassuring squeeze. "Yea, I'm fine. Just thinking about Tom, I guess." Giving him a weak smile as I moved my hand, "Hope he's okay. I hope Jude is too. We haven't known him *that* long, but it's bizarre to see him not himself. You know what I mean?"

Carder gave me a nod. "His quirkiness is running a little low right now, understandable, though. I'm sure Tom will be okay. He'll probably feel a hundred times better when he realizes Jude is there with him."

That gave me some hope. Carder was awfully good at delivering that when it was needed. And he was also good at helping to fill the time; we spotted a bookshelf in the waiting room full of books, board games, puzzles, dully colored building blocks, and coloring books.

Carder gestured to the *Battleship* game, to which I naturally gave him a glare and a matching playful punch in the arm.

Too soon.

Still not over that ridiculous game session we had.

I mean,

it was genius to not put any of his ships down,

but evil.

We settled on a puzzle that was already out on a table and partially started. As we agreed and sat down in the pieces' company, I wondered if the person or people who began the puzzle voyage either departed out of boredom, extremely poor circumstances left them with no reason to be there, or good health found its way to whomever they were there for. Whoever it was, I hope it was the last one.

Carder and I got quite invested in the puzzle quickly. I hadn't noticed we weren't really talking anymore. Our communication had been solely reduced to pointing at pieces.

A shared glance, an exaggerated shrug of the shoulders when a piece didn't fit that we thought for sure would, or a disapproving glance when the other was trying to stick a piece that they knew wouldn't work but insisted on trying multiple times anyway.

Carder.

I am describing Carder,

that stubborn puzzler.

The cover of the puzzle box sat in front of us, every couple of pieces I would touch, I found my eyes reverting to its picture. In majestic type letters, the box read, *A Pause in Autumn*. This particular fictional moment captured in hypothetical time was a quaint little cottage with beautifully full trees rocking some orange, red, and yellow leaves. Two chairs on the front porch, two sets of shoes outside the door, and a swing decorated one of the large trees. It looked like whoever took up residency here had it pretty good. I wished I could take the same pause; that was probably the whole idea behind whoever designed this puzzle.

I wonder about the handful of people in this world who can actually write down on their resume that they are indeed a professional puzzle designer.

Vibrate

Sherlock: *I think I should stay here with Tom. I can't bear to leave him anywho, even if he said I should go... I'm terribly sorry. I feel bad that you and Carder are just sitting in there.*

I snapped a quick picture of Carder, who is hyper-focused on a particular group of puzzle pieces, to Jude and sent a message along with it.

Me: *I think you're right. You should stay with Tom. Carder and I are perfectly entertained right now; no worries over here.*

Carder hadn't noticed I took a picture, or he did, and he's silently pleased he's been candidly photographed.

Sherlock: *Those puzzle pieces don't stand a chance against you guys, you'll put them in their place. I don't want to come across as rude; I'm really sorry. I just don't want to leave Tom's side right now. And I feel quite bad that you guys are there. If you'd like to go home, please do; you probably would like to rest in your own bed or something. Perhaps Alan could pick you guys up, or I could get a cab for you both?*

I looked over Jude's message, contemplating before I gently nudged Carder pulling him out of his puzzle trance. "Jude texted me that he's going to stay with Tom, which I think is best. He said he feels bad that we're just sitting here, and if we'd like, we can go home. What do you wanna do?"

Carder also contemplated for a moment, "Lucy, please, I am far too invested in this puzzle to leave." Without a blink of his sassy eyes, his full attention was returned to the adrift pieces.

Not much discussion there.

Me: *Carder is pretty determined to finish this puzzle. We may be here awhile.*

I was hoping that response would at least make him smile a little. I think it will. I also think it may bring him some comfort to know that while he's making sure Tom doesn't feel alone and he's supported that Carder and I are doing the same for him, even if we aren't in the same room.

Sherlock: *Please do send me picture updates on your puzzle progress or any waiting room shenanigans you may come across!*

Well, that made me smile. I could see the bit of dork in him coming out through his message. It was a refreshing and much-needed dose of Jude-dorkiness.

Carder was utterly immersed in his puzzle mission, and I felt a little heavy-eyed. So I decided to set up camp on the loveseat, also occupying the room.

Laying down on the somewhat comfy temporary bed, I felt like all my thoughts nestled right in with me. And they were heavy and not shy to really squeeze their way in and get comfortable.

Not all the thoughts were terrible; I guess it was a mixture of just everything.

Moments from the New York trip,

Or, just plainly, I went to New York and left Virginia Beach without Colin.

Well, now I'm also thinking about Colin.

I think he would have liked New York,

Definitely would have loved Coney Island.

Oh my gosh, he would have exploded excitedly seeing Jude's house and room.

Colin and Jude would have kicked it off, I think.

We would have had quite a little group, the four of us.

There's never really been a four of us.

The mystery of the playing card was looming over me as well. It's just so fricken odd and eerie, to be honest.

What in the hell was it supposed to mean, and why was it even there? And in Carder's slashed tire, it was almost like a message how could it not be? Slashing tires is such an aggressive and hostile thing to do, and the card was shoved in there.

It could have been missed, but it was found. I found it. Whoever did that must have wanted to be noticed to some extent.

I really feel like I should tell Carder about it at some point, I have to.

Is now the right time for that?

Although I don't even know if I would get much attention out of him right now with his heart deadset on that puzzle.

Although, it is drama we're talking about. That is a fair competitor.

I sat up and looked over at him. He was observing a few different pieces. "Hey, Carder?" I quietly called over to him. I'm not entirely sure why; it seems like unspoken waiting room etiquette.

"Yes, my Lucy-Lou?" He responded pleasantly, holding up two different puzzle pieces in the air and looking at their details with all the seriousness in the world.

"I hate pulling you away from your important business, which is not sarcasm. I actually really admire this devotion you've given *A Pause in Autumn-*"

"It deserves the justice of being finished," He stated without turning away from his precious pieces.

This made me giggle a little; just how abruptly passionate he sometimes gets. "Yes, I couldn't agree more. It is a beauty. I was just wondering if we could talk for a little while, and then I will return you to your mission. Only if that's okay. I don't want to,"

Before I could get another word in, Carder had left the pieces and sat on the other end of the loveseat. He was sitting with his back against the rest, and his legs extended as I copied him.

I gave him a little relieved smile of thanks. My mind tried to subconsciously calculate how many times we'd sat in this position. And how many conversations and topics that added up to as well, and all the different seats they had taken place on.

Before I dove into revealing the mystery, my eyes glanced over to the puzzle pieces that had been left yet again. I wish I could assure them that their faithful puzzler would be returned soon.

15. His Word 

I couldn't see if he was baffled or upset with me that I didn't tell him about this earlier; maybe he was a combination of both.

Which I couldn't really blame him.

It was in his slashed car tire it was found in.

Geez,

I can't believe that actually happened.

Carder took a moment to get his thoughts together. I could see them shuffling in his mind in the glaze of his slightly confused eyes. Once they were, apparently, gathered, he nudged his foot a little on my leg to get my attention.

I was anxiously zoning out while waiting for his response.

"This is freakin' weird." His words came out in a tone that sounded like he had made a grand discovery. "So, you were being a little snoopy snoop at Sherlock's house, huh?" He had his little mischievous smirk on, which was greeted with a glare from me.

"Jude. And I wasn't intentionally snooping. It just caught my eye and stuck with me for some reason. Or at least up until the point when I found that card in your tire. I don't know if it's the same exact card, but they're both the King of Hearts, and the card's design is scratched off the back."

"Yea, so like I said, this is flippin' weird." He scooted down a little, getting comfier.

By this action, I was a little worried about the puzzle pieces. I didn't want us to forget about them like others had. Goodness, Lucy, they're puzzle pieces. Stop projecting.

Carder's following words broke me from my puzzled puzzle concerns. "Do you think Seth has something to do with this?"

Now I was the confused one. "What?" Our eyes met with mutual conspiracy. "How could Seth be a part of this?"

"Tell me this doesn't sound like a Seth thing to do. With his crazy ass. You're finally living your life and leaving not only the city but also the state. And you were 'originally' going to do that for the first time with him when we graduated high school. He was probably trying to stop you; Seth knows where the apartment is because he helped you move here in the first place, and I've had the same car forever. My poor beauty, he's a psycho-"

"Okay, we can declare that a fact for sure. But Seth didn't know about the New York plans or anything like that. I'm afraid this ex-boyfriend theory, though it makes sense up until that little detail, does not fit. Must be something else."

Carder let out a sigh that was wearing just a tiny accent of frustration. "Well, we should tell Sherlock; we should be transparent about this jumbled-up chaos."

I sat up a little bit. "Jude. Why do you keep saying, Sherlock? And with the whole Tom thing, I don't think it's good timing. I wasn't even going to bring it up; I just felt like I couldn't hold it in anymore."

"You weren't going to tell me at all?" The accent of frustration turned to an undertone of hurt.

My eyes took a long blink as I felt a pit in my stomach. "I'm sorry, that's not what I meant to say. I was going to tell you eventually, of course, because you're my best friend. I just-"

Carder said something quietly under his breath, which was entirely out of the context of what makes Carder, Carder.

"I'm sorry I didn't really hear you; what did you say?" It felt weird saying that sentence to him. I didn't even know what tone to have or how to articulate that question.

"I said" He sounded sad. "It doesn't exactly feel like we're best friends anymore," he was sad.

And I was confused. Of course he's my best friend? That would never ever change.

"Our energy has just felt a little different, I guess, and I don't know."

I felt my heart hanging on the edge of anticipation.

"I'm probably just being dramatic, we've had a lot to process, and we had a long trip back; it would be nice to just go and sleep in our actual beds." Carder pulled out his phone to, I'm assuming, get us a ride as he carefully moved into a regular sitting position. "If you'd like to stay here, you can."

I didn't really know what to do.

I didn't know if he wanted me to come with him,

If he wanted to talk about all of this more,

Or if I had done something wrong.

I thought everything between us was okay?

I was back to feeling confused and new theories tossed in my head.

Ultimately neither of us really said much. This felt like a new feeling, and I didn't really care for it. It felt uneasy, and we should probably just have unpacked it and talked, but apparently, neither of us knew what to say.

Maybe we did just need sleep and unspoken space. I decided to stay in case Carder needed some time alone, which is understandable. Like he said, we have had to process a lot, and we had a long and weird trip back. Not to mention he's probably stressed about replacing his car tires; those damn things are expensive.

As Carder left, the thought of hope popped into my brain: I hope he feels okay soon and gets some good sleep. And I hope he knows, on the front lines and in the background chaos of his thoughts, that he is my best friend. He always will be.

The waiting room settled with a new atmosphere from Carder's absence. Emotional atmosphere, I should say. The physical presence of the space didn't shift, but the way it felt did.

I just realized that the puzzle pieces really were left behind again like I had feared they might be.

If I had just kept the stupid card to myself,

Carder would still be over there examining the pieces like he was viewing diamonds closely for their worth.

He'd probably have another decent chunk of it done, eventually the whole thing.

And I would have taken a victory picture of him and the completed puzzle. Like a parent takes a photo of their child with their cake on their birthday or with a trophy.

But now, the pieces remain scattered, incomplete, and rejected.

Why did I care so much about this puzzle, these pieces of cardboard with a glossy printed image that wasn't even within my radar of existence until we entered this room and gave it the smallest of attention?

It felt like the room had grown dim, and my thoughts had wandered to the light switch of my mind and dimed it as well, as my thoughts had a painful realization. This waiting room felt familiar; not that I had been in this exact one before, but one much like it.

The last time I was in one like this, I felt alone and abandoned, just like those puzzle pieces.

On the worst night of my life;

the night Colin left.

I can't even bear to say the actual word,

or how Colin left this world.

He left this world-

There's still a piece of me that believes in that pocket of time, he had changed his mind and didn't really want to leave. That's why he didn't struggle as much when I picked him up and ran with him to the hospital.

Well, that and he was probably too weak.

And now I am too weak in my mind and thoughts to not be pushed back into that memory.

With the rain continuing to downpour on us, I picked him up with my eyes blurry from my tears, and I brought him to the hospital as quickly as I could.

I hadn't remembered the look on the nurses' faces when I ran through the ER entrance until now; it was beginning to surface.

A dozen snippets from that night surfaced, sitting in this waiting room just as I sat in the hospital that night all by myself.

I remember I could hardly speak; I felt like I was going to throw up if I talked at all. I couldn't break my concentration from the floor as I stared at my wet shoes, and my thumb was digging into my opposite palm.

I could hear what the nurses and doctors were saying and asking.

But I could hardly reply.

They quickly switched their extensive questions to yes or no questions. I wrote down Colin's full name for them.

I couldn't say his name out loud.

It actually took me a really long time to be able to say Colin's name again.

My parents were called; they obviously found their contact info under Colin's emergency contacts in his file or whatever.

My parents.

My poor parents.

The sounds that came from them haunted me for the longest time, and I hated that I could hear it now.

Mom kept screaming Colin's name and shouting orphaned questions to the fluorescent lights.

I thought she'd never run out of energy to cry and yell, but eventually, it drained too much from her. She softly cried while she held him and rubbed his wet hair.

I remember thinking how weird it was that he was gone and his hair was wet, then I felt my own hair, and it was wet, and I thought this was the last present, situational, thing we would have in common.

Both of my parents were obviously, heartbreakingly distraught and destroyed. There is no competition of which parent was in mourning more or hurt, but seeing my Dad like that made my heartbreak even deeper.

It still does every time my mind recalls it. Dad's eyes were desperate as tears streamed down his shocked face, and eventually, his facial expressions became just- sad. More profound, more painful than sad, but just utterly and completely broken.

I remained in my chair,

I couldn't move.

A part of me felt like my parents blamed me for what happened.

Had I only gotten there sooner?

Why wasn't I home?

How could I not have known he was this depressed?

Why wasn't I there for him?

Why wasn't I there for my baby brother?

But my parents didn't blame me.

Maybe inside, they blamed themselves, but I'm not entirely sure.

I just know that they came over to me and comforted me once this earthquake settled just a little for them to remember they were still my parents, and I needed them.

I had lost my first and very best friend,

my only sibling,

the person who knew me inside and out;

and I had found him like that,

and I tried to save him from that.

That was the longest night of my life.

I never talk or really think about Colin's funeral like my mind will allow me to think and talk about the worst night. I just can't bring myself to do it.

Maybe because it was the last thing we could do for him. More so because it was the most depressing thing in the world to have a funeral for a teenage boy who didn't see the promise and light he held within him. Or maybe, as I am thinking about it now, I'm not being honest with myself. Perhaps I didn't talk about the funeral because I was angry with him and never told anyone that.

Not my parents.

Not Carder.

Not Seth.

No one.

I hardly admitted it to myself.

I was angry that he planned to do this but did it, knowing that I was very likely to be the one to find him. Then even worse, as a result of his actions, I tried my best to save him, and I failed.

I failed, and at his request, I gave him the comfort of singing our special song to him, but why didn't he tell me something to comfort me?

Why did he have to do this at all?

I was angry that he left me, and it wasn't until a few months later, within my grieving, did I realize that in his mind, I was leaving him by going to school out of state, and he felt alone in the world.

In reality, he wasn't. We would have made it through; we would both be in California right now.

But eventually, I stopped being mad at him and just missed him.

I missed the shit out of him.

And that was the replaced emotion associated with him from there on out.

My little brother.

Colin Houston MacArthur.

The Doctor to my Companion.

The young man who wrote a book he'd never see published or hear what I think about it.

The young man who never walked across the stage and received his diploma.

The young man who o broke my parents', Carder's, and my heart with his last decision.

My little brother, I miss so freakin much.

My little brother, who committed-

"Lucy?" A soft knock followed my name. "Are you okay?" Along with a flicked-on small source of light.

A lamp,

those things are called lamps.

The room had been dark,

I was sitting in the dark;

lost in the tidal wave of sad thoughts and memories.

Who knows how long I had been sitting like that?

Maybe I was partially asleep.

It would make sense with the nightmare of memories that often tackle my brain.

In any case, Jude came over next to me with concern clearly displayed on his tired face.

"I'm okay, just tired, I think. Are you okay? How's Tom doing?" I tried to snap out of the trance I still felt like I was in. Why does the past grab such a sharp hold?

"Tom is hanging in there. He will need a lot of rest, help, and recovery.

I'm worried about you, though; I think maybe you should head home and get some better rest? You look so tired."

Well, in my defense, I'm pretty sure I always look tired. But Jude was probably right. I just wish I could be alone in my head without this stuff circling in. A change of scenery may help with that, though. I gave him a nod.

After a minute on his phone, he gave my shoulder a quick enduring squeeze. "Alrighty, a cab should be here in a few minutes out front, don't worry about paying for it. I can't tell you how much I appreciate you and Carder and your support."

Oh, Carder, I hope he's feeling better.

"I'm really trying to keep it together,"

My eyes were brought to careful attention by his words.

"I'm so scared and worried for him, Lucy."

I didn't know if this was the right thing to do, but I stood up, which prompted him to as well, and I pulled Jude into a hug. Based on how caringly and long he hugged me back, I think I gave him what he needed. A brief and comforting pause from the hurt of reality.

Before we let go of our embrace and I made my way to the front of the hospital to catch my cab, I whispered a question to Jude.

"If you have time while Tom is sleeping or need a break outside his room, can you please try to finish this puzzle?"

Without hesitation or further question, he nodded. "You have my word." He gently pulled away so we could see each other's faces; I saw his smile for a split second.

16. Spontaneous Plateau

My life didn't feel like it had met a plateau for quite some time.

Well, ever since I met Jude.

Who was originally the mysterious bookstore guy,

then labeled as Sherlock for so long that it almost didn't feel necessary to discover his real name.

But then, it was indeed revealed and brought to a full circle-

Jude.

the still mysterious guy.

From the start, when Carder and I had become acquainted with him, life was moving in all sorts of adventurous and new directions. Not to say that our lives weren't bustling with their own day-to-day worries and endeavors before Jude came into the picture; just with him painted in, it felt different.

A good kind of different.

And now, in his absence, it felt like an odd different.

As of late, I have gotten close to radio silence from him.

Silence, perhaps in the form of busyness, but static nonetheless.

Dramatically, I must say, this plateau continues to exist.

A month in a half of spontaneous plateau.

That has got to be some kind of a complex oxymoron.

Spontaneous Plateau.

The last thing I received from Jude was a picture of the finished Autumn scene; he had fulfilled the puzzle's destiny as he said he would. It was amazing and funny at the same time to randomly get that picture. However, it probably would have been more satisfying to be a part of the construction process and see it in person. But still, I was both surprised and not surprised he made it a point to finish the puzzle after I so oddly asked him. That just seems to be in his character.

And Carder is still in and out of his typical character.

When I showed him the picture from Jude, he seemed less than impressed, like a split second of *'oh yea, look at that, Autumn,'* and that was about it.

I thought he'd genuinely be ecstatic that it was finished and not deserted, but I think he's just had other things on his mind lately that he isn't opening up to me about.

Throughout our friendship Carder hasn't really done that to me; he's usually pretty open with how he's feeling or if he's going through something. So, for him to be sheltering these feelings away from me, to see the shift in his presence and vibe, not only do I feel worried about him, but I feel like a terrible friend.

Was it something I did?

Was it something I didn't do?

Is there something I *can* do?

What can I do to see my marvelous sarcastic wonderful best friend again–

Where is my Carder?

Even at work, he hasn't entirely been the same.

We returned to our shifts the day after returning from New York. Alan had coffees waiting for us, which I was obviously excited about, and impressed that he nailed both of our orders.

I was looking forward to seeing Books & Such renovations.

Carder showed his gratitude for the coffee and gave the shop a glance before shuffling back into the routines of our oh-so-hectic positions as independent bookstore clerks.

Not even a single comment on the store's new layout and the fresh mustard yellow carpet Alan and Maybell apparently had their hearts set on. I have a hunch Alan suggested this carpet idea to Maybell, intending to poke Carder's sassy fire, but if that was the case, the mission has thus far failed.

At the time, I was taken aback, as was Alan, who was fully prepared to take some playful jabs and hear all about our adventure to NYC.

Alan and I ended up talking a bit later about the trip. How the Ferris Wheel totally stopped working because some worker won the lottery and walked off the job. How ginormous the Johnson's house was, and the beauty of the wedding day. I also thanked him for being there for Tom and expressed my sincere worries about how scary that must have been.

I learned then how loyal, and genuinely selfless Alan is to the people he cares about.

Alan acted like it was no big deal and was glad he was there. And I could see he truly meant all of it. However, it was a little hard at times to fully take in everything he said with complete seriousness as he was, with all the gravity in the world, stroking his *'beard.'*

I'll never understand that, but hey if it makes him happy let the artificial hair fibers live on man.

Carder's just been kind of coasting along ever since we got back from New York. I know sometimes getting back into the groove of everyday things post-vacation can take a while. And then, on top of that, all the news that's come into our orbit. Still, he really seems to be lost in space somewhere. And I can't seem to find him.

In today's case, though, the Universe declared we receive yet another impromptu break. Our shift ended early because the store's lights started to freak out. I guess the electrician who came during the renovations will have to take another trip over to Books & Such.

Based on Carder's facial expression when we got off the phone with Alan and explained the light situation, we weren't super disappointed with the fact.

I could use a nice coffee and a lazy session. It feels like a lazy coffee kind of afternoon.

The atmosphere changed as we came home from work, and Carder checked his phone while I was about to make some coffee for my soon-to-be lazy bones.

"Holy shit."

I turned from the coffee grounds to see Carder looking at his phone with, dare I say, a speck of excitement in his eyes.

"Put those grounds down, my little coffee addict. We've just been invited to dinner." Carder's eyes peeled away from his phone, and it felt like so long since we had connected enthusiasm through our facial expressions.

I didn't want it to end. "It's going to take quite the invitation to get me to put these grounds down." Giving him some sassy banter, I missed dishing it out, and I'm sure he missed receiving it. "Might I ask whom we have been asked to dine with?" Exchanging my sass for an abysmal British accent.

"We have been invited to dine with none other than the utmost interestingly insane delightful human this outlandish world has mustered up."

Goodness, not only was his accent way better, but just to whip out that vocabulary- he was more than ready, he delivered. And the suspense is killing me!

"Auntie Figgy is in town." His accent eased my anticipation with the sly smirk I dearly missed.

There's my Carder.

17. Desired Existence

"**W**ait," My giddiness caught up to my realization, "*Thee* Auntie Figgy?"

"Yes, the wonderful-wild-beautiful-hippie bitch herself, she is BACK!"

"Carder, really, should you be calling your Aunt a bitch?"

He promptly showed me the message she sent him indicating she was back in town; it was a link to *Sir Elton John's* magnificent song *'The Bitch is Back.'*

"Huh, okay, I rest my case. And we should definitely listen to this song while we're getting ready."

"Oh, Darling, it's already being done," Carder gave me a sly smile as the song began to play through his phone. "Now, let's go get ready, 80's-teenag-ers-montage style."

And with a pull of my hand, we were running down the hall as he departed to his room and I to mine. He kept the door open, though, so the 'soundtrack' to our spontaneous montage could blast on.

Auntie Figgy is the hippie haven Carder was thankfully able to run to when his douchebag parents disowned him after he came out.

My understanding of her from the vast stories Carder monologed and retold and my brief interactions with her is that she is always on an adventure somewhere.

So, when Carder needed a place to go, she put adventuring on pause for a while so he felt like he had a home again. Once Carder felt at home and comfortable enough to be alone, which ultimately, he just ended up at my house all the time anyway, she was off on her adventures again.

I believe she had been gone for the past year or so, hiking the Appalachian Trail for the second time.

Or the third.

Who knows!

That actually wouldn't surprise me.

The trail is roughly 2,200 miles from Georgia to Maine, and lots of characters along the way, I'm sure.

Oh man, dinner will be so fun with all the stories she must have just from her latest adventure alone! I'm looking forward to being in the house again; I haven't spent much time there because Carder usually just came to my house growing up.

Or me, him, and Colin were off somewhere. He also moved in with his ex-Jason shortly after turning 18, which didn't bother Aunt Figgy.

To her, the house was just a place for her to rest for a few weeks or so in-between journeys. It would be there regardless of who was or wasn't occupying it.

Now that I think of it, I wonder why Carder didn't just go back there when he left Jason's and why he came here?

Maybe he didn't want me to be alone,

or he didn't want to be alone.

Seems silly to ask him about it now.

Whatever the reasoning is, he ended up here where he belongs, and we've got some great Carder-Lucy moments out of it. He really is my best friend.

"LlluuUUuuUUccCccyyYyyy!"

Yepp, that's my best friend, alright.

Carder came swinging and singing into my room; mind you, the door was shut, and he didn't knock. Yet again, his playful hand found mine as his eyes matched the musical intensity of his following words "Let's dance." With a little raise of his eyebrow, he twirled me around, and our swing dancing moves were being utilized again.

Wow, that class really did pay off!

Music from Carder's phone that currently resided in his back pocket occupied the previous stillness of my room as we transformed it into a close-knit dance floor.

All of this sudden Carder-ness made me so giddy. It felt like old times. It felt like I was in a void filled with an air of carefree contentment with the 2nd person in my life who knows me best. I'd only felt this void with the person who knows me the best; that's Colin.

I hate using past tense with him; sometimes I don't.

Once our dancing session was done and we got into our dinner outfits, we headed out the door to the magnificent Auntie Figgy's.

The jam out continued on the way over as Carder chimed in-between iconic lyrics to express his excitement. "It's been so long since I've seen that fabulous-bohemian-wondrously-organized-mess of a human being!" He sang over the music with wide eyes, like he was in line for a ride he's heard about all summer long and finally got the opportunity to go on.

I raised my eyebrows in amusement at his long, playful, yet fitting description. "Yea, seriously, I'm like semi-nervous, but then I remember she's probably one of the most laidback people I've ever met."

"Precisely, that woman is a Saint-"

Just at the end of his righteous word, he laid on his horn and said some vulgar words to a car in front of us.

"And I did not inherit that from her."

We both laughed together, which felt so natural and right.

And Carder sped up and got in front of his nemesis car, which naturally made me slide a little to the left.

Oh, Carder, what an angry comedic driver you are.

Pulling up to Auntie Figgy's was pure nostalgia, more so for Carder, but it felt weird and lovely simultaneously. The last time I pulled up in a car to this house was with the same driver, but we had another passenger. Before my mind could trail much deeper into that, Carder, as he always unknowingly does, lovingly pulled me back into reality with a touch of his hand. Looking over at him, he had such a broad smile pastured on his face. It would be a crime against happiness not to mimic the closest I authentically can.

And so, I did, and it was either convincing or tolerated as we got out of the car and headed for the red front door.

Until Carder had knocked, I completely forgot they had a special knock between the two of them.

He knocks in the beat of the first half of the chorus to Madonna's 'Material Girl,' and she knocks in the rhythm to the other half before opening the door.

And my goodness, the amount of squealed excitement that came from both sides of the door while this occurred was adorable to witness. As soon as the door opened and Auntie Figgy's peaceful yet energized presence was before us, I think we both just felt a wave of serenity.

She gave us this sly smile while she put her hands in the air as if she was a model on a gameshow and showing off the grand showcase prize, which was indeed her presence. As she finally uttered her famous greeting, "Salutations, Aliens."

Auntie Figgy sealed it with a wink, and I swear we both felt in the warm light of a celebrity.

Motioning us inside, it was like we were departing from the reality of Virginia Beach and entering the vast bohemian world that was waiting for us.

An aroma of lavender gently rushed through our noses, and my body already felt at ease looking at the comfy and colorful cushions scattered throughout the living room.

My stomach was a little more than excited to see the tasty side dishes residing in the dining room. Something I remember about Auntie Figgy was she certainly did not mess around when it came to food.

Figgy is a big foodie.

While entering the kitchen/dining room, we sat around the barely lifted table on the cushions provided in substitute of chairs.

That's right, chairs.

There's a new sitting object in town.

And its name is COZY CUSHION.

Auntie Figgy began explaining the large variety of sides we saw before us. She expressed her love of getting different recipes from people she meets on the hiking trails or hostels; my goodness, what an adventurous woman in every aspect.

I wonder if that ever gets exhausting, like she feels the expectation of adventure on her after all these years, so she feels obligated to be like: '*Yea, my original plan was to go stay in Spain for about two weeks, but I'll totally join this random person in their voyage of foraging for some weird edible plants that will probably take over a month to find, all because we had dinner once and it went fairly well, apparently.*'

Yes, that is an actual experience she has had.

Or, this is just her desired existence.

This is her way of life, and she knows no other way.

Was she always like this?

Or did something happen that made her switch her lifestyle and state of mind entirely, and now she says yes to everything?

I hope she writes a book someday that's either a memoir or a work of fiction heavily influenced by all her travels, stories, and life lessons. I'm sure everyone could take something away from the chaotic wonder that is Auntie Figgy.

Her book's title would be absolutely brilliant,

Or totally irrelevant.

There is literally no in-between.

"Carder, my muse, I have been looking forward to seeing that beautiful face. Look, I brought out the Turkish Coffee; that way, you can really see how much I've dearly missed you." Auntie Figgy cunningly smiled at me and indicated with a swift wink that it will indeed never get old to shower Carder in both compliments and sass. She poured us each a small cup of Turkish Coffee.

And at the sound of the coffee hitting the glass, I could feel my smile get five times wider.

"Alright, you've got your coffee, and I have an abundance of food before us; now, I want some details on your lives." She turned from Carder to me. "Are you still seeing that, fella?"

My eyes got wide, as I was not expecting that. Man, Auntie Figgy really has been gone for a long time.

Hesitantly I opened my mouth to answer, but just like Carder, she beat me to it. "I didn't think so, and if I may say so, I'm glad. Your whole aura is brighter, as it should be." She gave me a sweet smile, one that kind of reminded me of my Mom.

Before she even blinked, she faced Carder with a different tone across her body language. "And you," She was getting down to business, "Your whole aura is mixed and thrown. What's going on with you?" Well, down to business but with a hint of genuine love and concern.

I also looked at Carder with subtle curiosity. He has been acting differently lately, but I also felt a little guilty, like he was being put on the spot.

He sassily scoffed, "Oh please, I am simply always evolving; keep up, Figgy." Taking a sip of his coffee as she laughed and agreed that we are all ever-growing beings. "Some things have changed, though; you know that Jason and I broke up from that postcard I sent you, which I am still bewildered that it even got to you. That was a postal worker miracle."

Altogether we took a moment of silent humming, per Auntie Figgy's request, in our deepest gratitude for postal workers everywhere.

"Alright, where was I," Carder brought us back to the conversation. "Oh! And I moved in with Lucy. It's been really nice."

We mirrored a smile to one another; I could see Auntie Figgy's grin from the corner of my eye at our interaction.

"We also took a trip to New York City a few weeks ago. We attended a wedding- Figgy, you would not believe the luxury of this flippin' house. It was insane!"

My own thoughts kind of started to play over Carder reminiscing about our trip. Not that I wasn't interested; sometimes, my mind just does that.

I started thinking about the playing card stuffed in the slashed tire. Then the adventure of exploring the Johnson's house.

Hearing Jude play piano and falling asleep in his room.

The ping-pong tournament, the ceremony, when Carder kissed me-

"I think my favorite part, besides the wedding, naturally, was wandering around Coney Island. How about you, Lucy-Lou?"

Carder's question snapped me out of my own montage; thankful I was chimed in on a relatively easy question. "It's tough to pick out just one thing. I think the whole trip was an exciting experience; I just liked being in the good company of Carder and Jude."

"Jude, I'm guessing a fellow traveling companion?" Auntie Figgy questioned, as I then questioned inside my mind why Carder didn't mention him when he's the whole reason why we went to New York in the first place?

I started filling in the blanks of who Jude was, and before he was Jude, he was Sherlock and the storybook-like way we crossed paths. Maybe I got a little carried away; we just have a lot of funny moments and memories with him, and he's a new friend of ours. But I guess Carder didn't really care to weigh in on the topic because he got up to go to the restroom or something. When I realized he had gotten up and left the room by the sound of a door shutting across the house, I stopped talking for a moment.

"Oh, he's okay," Auntie Figgy gently placed one of her well-traveled hands on mine, "I think he's just a little jealous. He'll be fine."

As she returned her hand, I gave her a confused expression. "Jealous?"

"I've known Carder for a very long time. I've seen him flourish into new versions of himself. Some progressive, some a little rough around the edges, but in every version you were present in, I could see the positivity thrive within him. And I'd like to think I know him pretty well; I could tell he was off, but I wasn't sure what was bleeding in. But now this makes sense, he's never really been the envious or jealous type, but there's a touch of it in there."

Well, first off, I was astounded that she had any indication of that because I am about as insightful and oblivious as a caged bird with short-term memory.

Secondly, I was stunned that she thought he was jealous. Because I still couldn't wrap my head around what he would be jealous of.

Almost every time I hang out with Jude, Carder is there too, or he's at work.

And as of late, I haven't even hung out with or heard from Jude anyway.

Before I could ponder more, Carder came back into the room.

With all her chill depth, Auntie Figgy immediately took the reins of the conversation. She talked about the different dishes she had on the table, and with each one, she told the story of the person she got the recipe from. She was fascinating, as was each person she talked about.

I wonder what if I ever gave her a recipe and she shared that meal with someone what she would say about me.

Her perception of what the vibe needed was spot on; it felt so warm, welcoming, cozy, and just peacefully right to be talking and laughing. Auntie Figgy finished her second cup of Turkish Coffee and sighed wistfully. "I wonder how many dreams I've mustered up within these plastered walls." She looked around the room and kind of past the area we were in, taking in the atmosphere of her home. "It's been good to me, this little building, but Virginia Beach is not my final resting place. I'm not sure where I'll wash up, but I sure would like to have peace in knowing this place is passed along to someone who will appreciate its value and memories." She smiled at Carder and me. "Perhaps I'm having dinner with them right now."

Just as I saw Carder's face light up and my smile widened, I felt my phone vibrate twice. Looking down at my phone to see I had received two texts. I could feel Carder looking in my direction, probably with the biggest smile he was hoping to share with me. But I couldn't peel my eyes off the screen, looking at the texts I received.

Sherlock: *Miss Lucy, I am terribly sorry I haven't been in greater contact with you and Carder. I've been so focused on helping Tom through rehab and being there for him and the marsh, but that is no excuse for my deep absence. I miss you.*

757-555-7823: *Hey Mac, can we talk?*

18. Sherlock & Watson

Me: *You don't have to be sorry, how is Tom doing? How are you doing? I miss you too.*

Sherlock: *Tom appears to be doing better some days, and others not so much. I think it helps bring him some peace, knowing that I'm there with him through this recovery. How have you and Carder been?*

Sherlock: *Miss Lucy, is everything okay?*

Me: *Yea, I'm sorry for my late response. Carder kind of seemed like he was upset with me. We were having dinner at his Aunt's house, and I got really excited to hear from you, so I guess I was on my phone a lot.*

Sherlock: *Oh I see, I apologize if I caused any harm or interruption.*

Me: *Oh no you didn't don't worry. Carder is just being sassy dramatic Carder.*

Sherlock: *He is notoriously gifted in the sass department, not to be taken lightly*

Me: *Okay that totally made me laugh, which made Carder glare at me, and I can't even tell him why I laughed a little because that* *will make the glare all the more intense and powerful*

Sherlock: *It would definitely create a mass glare which could cause, well, we don't even know what kind of damage. Best to lay low on laughing sources at this point.*

Sherlock: *In all seriousness though, you could just tell him we're texting, or I could shoot him a text? I miss you guys!*

Me: *Maybe give Carder some space, I don't know, he's been kind of off lately*

Sherlock: *Oh, I'm sorry to hear that- how do you mean?*

Me: *He just hasn't been acting like himself, well today he was because we were by his Aunt's and he got really excited to see her*

Me: *She's really cool, you'd like her a lot*

Me: *I actually mentioned you*

Me: *Anyway, his Aunt actually said maybe he's jealous but I'm not sure what he'd be jealous about?*

Sherlock: *Hmm, it seems she knows him pretty well, I'm not really sure what he would be jealous about either. Maybe you guys need a heart-to-heart?*

Sherlock: *You mentioned me, huh?*

Me: *That's a good idea, maybe that's what he needs, a nice binging session of a great show. We found out at the wedding that he loves wine, and some bestie talk*

Me: *Maybe*

Me: *Yes I did*

Me: *Not relevant*

Sherlock: *I sure hope that helps patch things up between you both, please do keep me informed!*

Sherlock: *Ah yes the wedding, we actually didn't even really get to talk about it that much. Did you have a nice time?*

Sherlock: *Hmm, seems relevant to me*

Me: *Will do on operation bring Carder home, I've decided that's what we'll call it*

Me: *Wow I didn't realize we didn't really talk about the wedding together, it's been a crazy couple of weeks! I had a great time, I'm really happy for Julia and Angelo. Have you heard from them at all? How's their Honeymoon going?*

Me: *Psshhhh nooooooooooo*

Sherlock: *Good call, this is why you're head of operation naming*

Sherlock: *I'm so glad you enjoyed it, yes I have heard from them! They are doing wonderfully, they both missed Italy a lot. I mean who wouldn't, and I've gotten some great pictures. Quite the pair those two are, I hope to be lucky like them someday.*

Sherlock: *You only deepen my curiosity by your anticipation, but I shall not press and will therefore let it go*

Me: *Awwww that's amazing! I'm really happy to hear that, they deserve it*

Oh I'm sure you will find your special someone one day, and they will be awfully lucky!

Me: *It's hard to tell you embarrassing things when you talk so elegantly, damn you and your poise!*

Me: *Haha just kidding*

Sherlock: *Why do you say that?*

Me: *Saaayyyy what*

Sherlock: *That the 'special someone' would be awfully lucky?*

Me: *You're just a really kind, cool, and an awesome person. You're so full of life and stories, I just feel like whoever you share your life with its bound to be pretty amazing*

Me: *Sorry if that was a bit much*

Sherlock: *Oh no Miss Lucy, that was so very nice to read and I am keeping it close to my heart, thank you. I had to go check on Tom and help him a bit, I'm sorry for my late response!*

Me: *Phew okay haha I thought I may have made things awkward or something*

Sherlock: *You're chatting with the ambassador of awkwardness, everything is a-okay*

Me: *Ambassador of Awkwardness, I am so changing that to your name in my phone*

Ambassador of Awkwardness: *That is a pretty snappy title, I can't even lie*

Me: *Haha okay just kidding I'm changing it, Ambassador of Awkwardness is too long to keep seeing in my notifications haha*

Jude: *Ah yes that would get a tad annoying, what is it now?*

Me: *Your name but of course*

Jude: *Sherlock?*

Me: *Noooooo*

Me: *Jude*

Me: *Silly*

Jude: *Oh, I thought I was your Sherlock*

Jude: *I liked being him*

Me: *You still are haha*

Jude: *Remember when we first met? Seems like a really long time ago*

Me: *Yea it really does, I can't believe I ran into that bookshelf and cut my forehead oh my gosh haha*

Jude: *I was so stunned! But happy that I could help you pick up the books and then read to you a bit, that was exhilerating*

Me: *I dare say you are quite the bold gentlemen*

Jude: *Honestly I never really was that way, it was just something about you that made me want to be*

Jude: *Speaking of bold*

Jude: *Have you had any coffee today?*

Me: *I don't think I would be functioning without having some coffee in my system. Auntie Figgy gave us some delicious Turkish Coffee*

Me: *Buuuuuuuuut if you're asking if I'd like mooooore coffee the answer is always yes*

757-555-7823: *Mac, I seriously need to talk to you*

Jude: *Your deductions are correct Watson, I was going to ask if you'd like to get some coffee and perhaps go for a short walk?*

Me: *Sorry for the pause, we were saying our goodbyes and got home a little while ago*

Me: *I just checked in on Carder, I think he's taking a nap right now so maybe when I get back I can have that heart to heart with him*

Me: *Let's go get some coffee!*

Jude: *Sounds perfect to me!*

757-555-7823: *This isn't funny I know you're getting my texts*

757-555-7823: *You really need to answer*

757-555-7823: *We need to talk*

757-555-7823: *Please Mac*

19. Shifted

Me: *Seth. Do NOT call me mac and STOP texting me.*

After quietly leaving the apartment to avoid a slumbering Carder, I started my short walk to meet Jude for coffee.

Wow, so much coffee in one day.

When a day has coffee, can that day really be poor?

And coffee in the company of a good friend, why that's even better.

I saw him sitting at a table, waiting for me through the glass door. To the reaction of me opening it, I was presented with the goony smile I missed more than I had anticipated. And to my surprise, Jude stood up and walked over to me to give me a warm hug.

Well,

I'm not *super* surprised.

He is quite the gentleman.

The hug was a tad bit longer than I thought it would be. But, by the time I was wondering how long our hug had been and how long a 'standard' hug typically is, we let go and sat down, where I was pleasantly surprised again.

And with all his Sherlockness, he noticed. "If you'd like a different drink, I can totally get you one," he gestured to the coffee cup that was waiting patiently for me. "I just couldn't think of a higher honor I could be bestowed upon today than to drink some coffee with you. When I got here, I thought that, indeed, there was a higher honor I could achieve- buying you a coffee! I was going to wait until you got here,"

He's rambling already, "Jude." The ramble never fails to make me grin.

"But then I thought maybe I could surprise you, but by the time I had placed the order I-"

"Jude," I placed my hand on his for a moment to seize his thoughts, but it seemed I may have seized his whole body by the smooth shift in his lightly smiling eyes.

"Sorry," he said with his little crooked smile, "Rambling again."

"It's okay," Smiling and bringing my hand back and greeting it with the warm glass that generously held the magical black bean juice. "I'm sure this coffee is great; I trust your caffeinated judgment. Thank you very much for getting it for me."

"Absolutely, Miss Lucy, without question." His smile was noticeably occupied in his thoughts, and I saw the tiniest hint of a blush creeping up his cheeks. "This reminds me of when we went to the Café of Blues."

"Hmm, you don't say; which time are you recalling?"

"The second time, where I revealed my name to you via wallpaper."

Now that got an unexpected giggle out of me. "Okay, not many people can say a sentence like that. But yes, it is kind of reminding me of that night too. Sitting across from each other, drinking coffee, your smile seems about the same."

"Does it?" Jude's smile grew bigger at my sly compliment.

Oh yea, I still got it. Sort of.

"Gently, I must disagree; it feels brighter having grown closer to you."

It was my turn to blush a little, though I didn't really want to. "Speaking of which, let's talk about our trip that we totally went on and didn't even discuss- your sister got *married*!"

"And you left the city! No, not just the city; you left the STATE!" Jude shouted with enthusiasm, as the small population of fellow coffee drinkers didn't seem to care enough to investigate.

With shared laughter, we reminisced about the trip's little moments we particularly enjoyed.

Jude told me more about his maid of honor duties, and I told him about the badass ping pong tournament. He told me how much his heart filled with nostalgia and warmth when we discovered his room, and he played his piano again. I told him about the nausea and worry that filled my heart when the Ferris Wheel at Coney Island stopped. Now it's a pretty hilariously unique story, but it was pretty terrifying at the time.

"The wedding was stunning. I know my opinion doesn't mean a lot because that's the only wedding I've ever been to, but it was the prettiest and best wedding ever." Giving Jude a giddy smirk, remembering just how perfect the whole thing was for such a divine couple like Julia and Angelo.

And with that, he reflected my giddiness. "Indeed it was; everything turned out pretty grand for them. Julia is amazing, and Angelo is a real swell guy."

Oh my gosh, he is literally a 1920s cartoon character; he and his vocabulary.

"I was nervous about the ceremony, but I think it went smoothly! What did you think?"

"Oh, it was beautiful. Everything was so elegant, and though I don't know the couple that well, it seemed to reflect them marvelously. And you did a great job, Madam Maid of Honor."

Jude could not hide the happy color complimenting his face. And for some reason, the look in his eyes reminded me of Carder's when he kissed me after the ceremony.

"Why thank you, and I wear the title with the utmost honor, no pun intended."

The word pun brought my attention back, but I think he could tell I was zoned out. Who am I kidding? You bet your tobacco pipe and deerstalker, he noticed.

"Come in, Miss Lucy, come in," He jokingly radioed to me on his state-of-the-art imaginary walkie-talkie.

Promptly energized by the imagination he constantly brings out of me, I radioed him back. "Yes, I am still present, over." Adding on the best imitations of a walkie-talkie I could produce before letting the bit go. "I guess something popped into my mind that happened at the wedding. It's been popping in and out of my mind since then. I haven't really talked about it."

And I wasn't even sure if I should or wanted to.

Or why it was so confusing to me.

Am I making a big deal out of nothing?

Jude appeared puzzled, and rightfully so, with the change of conversation wrench I just threw. But as always, "Well, if you'd like to talk about it, I'm here for you." he provided a reassuring and kind space.

With a sharp inhale, I raddled off the moment, the kiss, clearly and quickly.

His smiley expression had shifted into a facial tone I couldn't read.

"Oh, I see, wow. And how did you feel about that? Do you think it was entirely serious?"

I shrugged. "Honestly, I have no idea. I've thought about it so much that it's become a boiling pot of overthinking. Maybe it isn't a serious thing that happened."

"But was it serious to you?"

Well damn, Jude, breaking out the Dr. Phil questions. "Well, I don't know," Trailing off a little, "If I kiss someone, it isn't random. It's because I want to, and I feel something for them. But that's just me. I don't know about Carder."

"I'm not sure about Carder either. I agree with you, though."

I looked up from my coffee cup, sometimes it looked like a little galaxy swirling about, and into those grey-blue eyes that I've seen quite a few emotions in but not quite this one.

"I wouldn't kiss someone unless I had their permission, and I felt deeply for them. And to be honest, at the wedding, I kind of wanted to kiss you."

I was shocked, to say the least.

I had no idea what to say.

And it was probably plainly painted all over my face.

"The atmosphere of a wedding and day of love certainly breaks out the hopeless romantics in people, huh?" He clicked his mug to mine and took a drink.

I was still a little too stunned to take a sip of mine.

Well, not right away.

But eventually, I did.

Come on, it's coffee.

On a more serious note, I didn't know if Jude was implying that he liked me more than a friend or if he and Carder were both just feeling under the spell of wedding day magic. For my sanity, I decided to proceed with the conversation as it seemed he was doing the same. And after that internal decision, I felt my phone vibrate.

Carder: *Did you go somewhere?*

"I think Carder must have sensed we were talking about him" I showed Jude my notification. "The Queen has awakened," I laughed and quickly replied to him. To which he was swift in replying back.

Me: *Just getting some coffee with Jude, I didn't want to wake you up in case you wanted to just sleep*

Carder: *A note or text or something would have been nice*

Carder: *I was worried about you*

Carder: *A weird number had been texting me asking me where you were, and I figured it was fricken Seth and then I got scared when I realized you weren't here*

Me: *He's messaging you? What a psycho, he's been messaging me too. I'm really sorry I scared you, I'll be home soon*

Carder: *See you soon*

"Sorry about that," Letting out a short sigh; my, the thumb exercise of fast texting.

"That's quite alright. Is everything okay with Carder?"

"Yea, yea, he's okay, thanks for asking," Setting my phone down on the table and bringing my hands back to the warmth of the coffee cup.

Jude brought us back to our reminiscing. "It was quite the crazy trip, filled with lots of moments and emotions, huh?" He philosophized, followed by a swig of his coffee.

I matched his sip in agreement. "Yea," the beginning of our trip started playing in my head. "It was pretty crazy."

I hate when you can tell your mood has kind of shifted. You don't want it to be noticeable because you aren't ready to address it yet. Still, the vibe radiates in the room; obviously, your company can tell.

So, do I confront it first, or wait for Jude to inevitably ask-

"Hey, um, Lucy, is everything okay?"

Yepp, precisely that.

I started thinking about the playing card.

The King of Hearts shoved in Carder's slashed tire.

That was so intentional.

It was done for a reason.

The King of Hearts-

Jude just said, hopeless romantics.

The King of Hearts has a sword through his head.

But no, why would Jude do that?

He wouldn't do that-

Would he do that?

A conspiracy flood; that's just what I needed right now.

My phone started to vibrate, which shook me out of my racing thoughts. It was Seth, again, he sent me a picture of us from years ago. "My ex keeps messaging me, and apparently, he's been messaging Carder too. He keeps saying we need to talk, and he won't leave me alone, and now he's sending me pictures of us."

I opened the message and passed my phone to Jude. "I don't know what he could possibly have to talk about, he was horrible to me, and I want nothing to do with him. He's really-" I noticed Jude was awfully immersed in the picture. "Jude?"

"This guy," Jude's voice sounded so different; it was soft yet, "is your ex?" scared.

I nodded in confusion; why was he suddenly acting so strange?

"This guy said he lived in my neighborhood. I ran into him on a walk once, and we talked every now and then."

My heart was racing. "Wai- What?" I was so confused I didn't understand.

Jude's eyes, facial expression, and voice portrayed how my mind felt- a racing panic. "Lucy, I didn't know this was your ex; I had no idea."

Seth has been closer to me than I even realized,

he's always one step ahead of me,

one move away from me.

He's already getting in my head again,

making me feel stupid for trusting anyone,

making me feel exposed because of his sneakiness.

How could I fully trust what Jude was saying,

how do I know for sure they aren't conspiring together for-

I don't even know what?

For goodness sake, I didn't even know Jude's real name for who knows how long!

What if when Jude finally decided to share his name, it was because he broke his friendship or deal with Seth because he was starting to like me?

'But how could someone like you, who's so flawed?'

Seth's really in my head now.

'That's why I'm here, Mac. That's why I've always been here.'

His voice was so disgustingly loud and hurtful

'To remind you.'

Echoing in my brain

'That it's you and me.'

And I can't turn it off.

'I'm the only one who'll love the monster you are.'

I can't turn it off.

'The monster who couldn't save her brother.'

I need to break out of this; I need to get away.

Grabbing my phone out of Jude's hand, I didn't know if he was talking or trying to stop me. Everything around me was blurred by adrenaline-infused confusion piercing through my skull and taking everything in me but my ability to run as a hostage.

I need to get home.

I need to get home.

I need to get home.

I need to get to Carder.

20. Spaghetti for Two 

I felt him everywhere, like he was watching me.

Waiting for me to trip and fall.

Or watching me race home in a panic.

Only for him to come sneaking in.

Why couldn't Seth just stay away?

Why did he have to come and muddle himself in the middle of my life again?

How can he still be so obsessed with the idea of us?

There is no us. There hardly was an us when we were an us.

It was mainly him controlling me and me blinded by his fog to believe it was love.

Seth has no right to be taking up energy in my life.

He has no right to crawl back into my mind.

I just needed to get to Carder, and everything will be alright.

My mind streamed with a harsh cocktail of anxiousness, confusion, and anger, with cubes of sadness floating in its mix as I rushed into the apartment.

I started to ease, being back in a safe space. I felt my knees want to give, and I was sweating like nobody's business.

Course, Carder made it his business as my heavy breathing, produced by a lack of exercise to a full-blown sprint, caught up with me and was quite loud. Alarming Carder to come out of his room and see what was going on.

My knees were tempting a visit to the floor as I was guided to the couch by Carder's haste navigation and equally quick questions.

"What happened? Did you run? You don't run. Something bad happened- Lucy, what happened?" One question and statement after another. Carder's hand touched my forehead in a nurturing manner, and I saw him trying not to be grossed out by the sweatiness.

No offense taken.

I'm a hot mess right now.

Minus the hot.

Well, temperature wise yes.

I don't care what I look like right now.

My life's script has been dramatically swapped out from Wes Anderson to M. Night Shyamalan.

Finally, I caught my breath, and my thoughts froze just long enough for me to formulate a response. "I think I'm having a panic attack; I just ran to you." At the release of my last word, I looked up to Carder and his worried eyes. "I just, ran to you."

We looked at each other for a moment; I'm guessing we both had an elevated heart rates from panic and anticipation.

Then he hugged me. "It's okay Lucy."

And it was a hug I melted into so fast, the antidote I needed at this moment to calm myself down.

"You're okay."

To make me feel-

"You're safe."

safe. Exactly.

A small cry lumped in my throat; I didn't want to give it the satisfaction of releasing, but I honestly didn't have the energy to fight it. Softly it exited, and softly Carder's hand rubbed my back. And as each gentle stride of his hand came back up and down, I was reminded of all the times Carder's been there.

Always.

Especially the bathtub night, which was replaying in my head as we sat in this current moment. The way he held me, I had never felt safer. But right now, it felt so different in this hug and the comfort in his hands and words. In a way I couldn't describe.

"Do you want to talk about it?" He asked me in a soft and patient tone.

I needed a second to answer, a second to be in this second. Because after this second, there was no promise things would feel the same. Although, whether we realize it or not, I think more seconds are like that than we notice, and we don't think to savor them.

Taking a calm breath, I began my dreaded embarkment outside the moment. "Seth won't stop trying to talk to me, he's been texting me a bunch, and he even sent me an old picture of us, whatever the hell that's supposed to mean. And I showed Jude when I got it, and he started acting weird. He pointed at Seth and asked me if that was my ex, and I said yes, and he got even weirder and panicky and started saying how he knew Seth, and it seemed like they were friends or something. Apparently, Jude ran into Seth on one of his walks around his new neighborhood. Seth lied and told Jude he was one of his neighbors, and they became friends."

As I was saying all this aloud, it made me analyze the situation more and feel even more confused. "I'm just so creeped out, and I don't even know what to think. I started thinking about the card in your tire and at Jude's house and how we thought maybe Seth had something to do with it, but that seemed impossible because he had no connection. But what if Jude was his connection? Either they met, and Seth convinced Jude to mess with me and sabotage things in my life so we would somehow get back together. But then Jude started becoming friends with us, so he wanted out. Or Seth tricked Jude and befriended him so he could always be a step ahead of me. But then, how'd Seth know where Jude lived?" I felt like a raging conspiracist.

Carder took a minute to absorb. "Okay, well, that is a lot of fuckery, goodness fuckin' gracious."

That's actually a pretty appropriate response to everything I just said.

"Sherlock doesn't seem like the type of person who would go along with someone asking him to purposely try to ruin someone else's life in the name of obsessive love. Then again, we didn't even know his real name for most of the time we knew him."

"That's what I was thinking! And we thought nothing of it! I just thought it was quirky!"

"We are suckers for quirky."

"Indubitably, and look where we are. We don't even know what to think! And Seth is out there with God knows how much information about me and what I've been doing."

"Well, it's probably safe to say that regardless of the relationship that Sherlock and Seth the douche had or have, Sherlock told Seth about our New York trip. And he's the one who tried to sabotage the trip by slashing my poor defenseless tires."

"It appears so" Oddly, a sense of calm overcame me. Not that I was okay with everything happening, but I think I felt better having told someone what was happening in my head. Especially the someone who means the most to me. "All these connecting the possible dots makes me kind of hungry."

"I'll make us some spaghetti," Carder said without skipping a beat and hopping off the couch, making his way to the kitchen, but not before giving me a kiss on the forehead.

"Why do you do that?" My curiosity blurted out, still on the high of bold conspiracies.

"Because I care about you, and it's cute to do," Carder responded from the kitchen as I heard cupboards open and close.

I let that sink in for a moment. "Hmm," But not too long. "Do you think you could please do something else cute for me?" Peeking over the couch into the kitchen to see my sassy chef look over his shoulder with a cocked eyebrow. "Could you please put on a pot of coffee I could wake up to? I feel like I'm hitting a wall; I may take just a little nap while you're cooking, if that's okay?"

Graciously and sassily, Carder gave me a nod and returned his attention back to the noodles he pulled out. "Probably all that sudden exercise you did."

We laughed at the facts, which became the segue into my swiftly approaching nap.

I must have been really sleepy to have drifted that fast.

And on the couch,

with no pillow or blanket.

Geez, Lucy.

Maybe you should exercise more.

Down down I went,

Cascade from each and every argument.

Down down I go,

Ditch reality far below.

My eyes opened, well, my dream eyes, per se.

I was in a living room on the couch, but not mine.

This was familiar, like I'd landed in this setting in dreams before.

Like the one I had quite a while ago where this was,

"Lucy, what shall we watch tonight?"

Colin's living room.

He walked in with a bowl of popcorn, smiling with curiosity awaiting my answer.

"Umm, I'm not sure. What are you in the mood for?" I asked him, feeling a little thrown off still. As much as it's happened to me, it's jarring to feel self-aware in your dreams.

Sitting down by me with the bowl of popcorn in the middle, Colin gave me an odd look. "TV time is on pause, something is on your mind, and this has just turned into a tea spill."

Laughing a little at his word choice, I couldn't deny how well he knew me and my clear body language. "I guess you're right, I just-" I looked Colin in the eyes, and this time it happened faster than it usually does when he appears in my dreams.

He knew I was dreaming. This wasn't real.

"Colin, I'm sorry I-"

"Lucy, your head is so loud and hurt."

My gosh, he looked so distraught.

"What's going on?"

I couldn't tell if he meant what had happened to him or what was currently happening with the Jude situation. "My life is just really messy right now, and honestly," Looking into those glossy eyes, I could still find some comfort, "I just wish you were here."

I could see the specks of guilt circulating in Colin's eyes as he tried to find the right words. He moved the bowl of popcorn on the coffee table and moved closer to me. "I guess that's why I come so often," His hand gravitated towards mine as our eyes were focused on other things. "Because I wish I was with you too."

I felt his hand on mine, then our eyes were at each other's attention once again.

He's aware then, in some sense, that he's only present in my dreams.

I could question this in a million different ways, how it's possible, how this could be, but I'm afraid if I speak them out loud, then I won't see him like this anymore.

When you miss someone so much, I guess it doesn't matter how you see them as long as you do.

"This friend that I made, that I'm pretty sure likes me, and I don't know if I have those feelings towards him or not. At times I felt like I did, but feeling that again is scary. Well, I'm unsure if I can trust him anymore or what to believe. Seth won't stop trying to talk to me, and part of that scares me, too, because he gets so drastic when his mind is set on something or doesn't get his way. And Carder, something is going on with Carder."

Out of the jumbled mess I just gave him, he picked the last thing to unpack. "What do you mean? What's going on with Carder?"

I shrugged as we let each other's hands go and got a little comfier on the couch. "Carder's just been acting a little different." Turning to Colin, a silly pondering question came out of me. "Do you think he likes me? Like more than a friend?" I knew it was a stupid question to ask, I was about to wave it off, but the look on Colin's face refrained me.

"I always thought there was something there, maybe not romantic in a traditional sense but in a life partner kind of way."

My stomach hastily opened the door to my heart that had just plummeted a few floors.

"I know that's probably not the answer you were expecting."

"No, not really," I responded in a blank and confused tone. "Why do you say that?"

Colin adjusted his posture more seriously. "Just the way he's always treated you, the way he looks at you, the way he speaks of you when you're not around. I mean, honestly, besides me, he's the one who knows you best in this world. He's always been there."

Colin said it all so well, with certainty and ease, almost like he had been waiting for this conversation.

Processing what he said, it all made sense, I suppose. It just felt strange to accept. "I guess I don't know what to do with that, you know?"

"I'm not saying I'm 100% correct either. But I'm usually pretty right." He gave me the worst attempt of a wink in the world, like brother like sister. "And you don't have to do anything with that. How do you feel?"

Pausing a moment, "I," something felt bright and pulling. "I feel," My eyes swung to Colin's, "I feel like I'm waking up."

I grabbed Colin's hand, thinking maybe if I held it tight enough, I wouldn't leave.

I felt centered with him.

I didn't want to leave again when I needed to hear more from him.

To be with him.

The brightness was growing, and I knew I was leaving. The look in Colin's eyes broke my heart. Even more than his last words before my eyes shot open.

"But I don't want you to wake up."

Carder was gently shaking my shoulder. "Spaghetti is ready sleepy Lucy-Lou."

21. Kitchen Sink 

I felt the weight of my dream press down on me as I sat up and got off the couch to follow Carder to our little kitchen table.

He had plates set out, the spaghetti ready to go, sides of bread, and a cup of coffee by my plate. Made just the way I like it.

Colin was right.

Besides him, Carder was the one who knew me best.

We sat and shared a meal and some laughs about how Carder managed to mess up spaghetti. It was just a tad bit sticky, but still, a delight to just be in each other's company and doing something slowed-down and normal.

I tried not to think about what Colin said in my dream, but it was hard not to.

"Has Sherlock or Seth tried messaging you again?" Carder suddenly asked.

"Um, I'm not sure. I haven't even checked my phone." Looking over to the couch where I apparently had left it, I went to check. I had received a few texts; two from Jude about an hour and a half ago and one from Seth about thirty minutes ago.

Jude: *I am truly sorry for the pain, anger, or confusion that has happened, please know that I am sincerely confused as well, and I'd really like to talk and figure this out. When you're ready, of course.*

Jude: *Lucy I am so so sorry*

757-555-7823: *I tried talking to you Mac, I wanted to talk to you. I really need you, and I was going to fix things. Know that this is your fault.*

Showing Carder the texts, he scoffed, but I wasn't sure to which one. "Seth is just trying to get a rise out of you, so you'll reply. If he doesn't stop, we need to file a harassment complaint or, better yet, just block his number or something."

"That's a good idea. I totally forgot you could do that." With a bit of hesitation initially because it was something I'd never done before, I went through with it and blocked his number. "Okay, it's done."

"Atta girl, that should give you peace of mind and keep that creep away."

"Yea, I think you're right."

Carder started cleaning up the plates and cooking stuff from dinner.

"What about Jude's messages?" I saw his steady movements pause and then proceed. "Maybe I was overthinking it, and he didn't know Seth was my ex. I could see Seth trying to pull off some craziness like that."

Carder shrugged his shoulders. "I mean, yeah, that's a possibility. Who knows?" I was thrown off by the sudden distance I could sense in his voice.

I struggled in my mind with the choice of addressing it or not. "Is something wrong? Are you okay?" Apparently, we are confronting it.

"I just feel like we talk about him a lot, about Sherlock."

"I didn't realize we did- and why do you still call him that?"

Carder dropped the dishes in the sink and turned towards me. "Because that's what he said his name was? And I didn't just fall in love with him and start calling him something else!"

He yelled; he was yelling at me.

I didn't even know how to react immediately. "First off, what're you talking about? Secondly," Goodness, this was hard to get through. I was so shaken. "Why in the world are you yelling at me?"

Carder took a deep breath and checked quickly if any of the dishes in the sink were broken. By his composure, I'm guessing not. "I guess I was holding that in for a long time, and it burst out, and I wasn't prepared for that. It just came out; I'm sorry I yelled at you. You didn't deserve that, and I really didn't mean to. I'm sorry Lucy."

Taking a moment to process, I nodded with my exhale. "I forgive you. I'm just confused."

Sincerely I did forgive him. It was hard to stay upset with him. "You've seemed off for a while now, and I've been trying to understand what's going on, and I should have just been more upfront and asked you."

Carder was looking at the floor. He hardly ever avoids eye contact when someone is talking to him. He loves attention.

"Carder, please tell me what's going on." My plea peeled his eyes off the floor and to me. "Please?"

I was still sitting in my chair as he leaned against the kitchen sink with his arms folded.

Carder almost looked nervous and unprepared, which made me feel the same. "Lucy," He said my name with a short pause, "I think you're the love of my life." His eyes looked at me.

Why, for a second, did my eyes not register them as my best friend's?

Because this felt like more than just uncharted territory.

This was the curve ball I never saw coming.

"Your standards make me sad," I responded in the best joking manner I could muster on the spot. My automatic reaction was to try to lighten the heavy mood that had settled between us. Because I couldn't bear the thought of some kind of weird tension between us. And I just can't handle confrontation or profound change right now, not after all the shit that's rolled out today.

"Lucy, come on, please I'm trying to be serious right now."

With that, I was silenced. I had no idea what to say.

"I love you, like in love with you. Not in a sexual way, I just- I don't know." Rubbing the back of his neck a little, his eye contact fleeted for a moment, as did mine.

"It was that moment at the wedding," he caught my eyes again. "When I kissed you, I acted on how I felt about you. Really, how I've always felt about you. I realized it fully on the day I was helping you get ready for the date of surprises Sherlock had planned for you. Truthfully, I've known it inside me since we got detention together in Middle School. I knew that you were my person. You're the person I want to riddle off every detail of my day to. You're the person I want to run to when I win a ping-pong tournament. You're the person I want to care for when they're not feeling well. And you are the person

I want to share this absurdly fantastical human experience with."

I felt even more intensity twist up in my chest with each word he said to me. "Carder, I don't understand, why would you- you're the one who practically threw me at Jude in the first place-"

"I know, I know I did I-"

"I didn't even know what I wanted or was ready for, and you pushed me to go on those dates or whatever you want to call them."

"Lucy, I know. I did that at the time because I wanted you to try something new, get back out there, and be happy. I just didn't realize that I wanted to be the one to give you that."

I had never witnessed Carder so vulnerable in my life, and to be quite frank, it was freaky.

"As you and Sherlock started to get closer, it seemed, I started catching myself getting kind of jealous and this odd annoyance towards him. I didn't want to have that reaction, he's not a bad guy, and he's helped bring you out of your shell more. I didn't understand why but then it clicked. I wanted to be the one to give you happiness because I love you and care about you, and I feel like I know you pretty damn well."

"That you do," I said blankly, which I felt kind of bad about, given how raw he was being, but I just didn't know what to do. "I don't know what to say. So much is happening right now- Why did- why did you have to say all that?"

"Excuse me?" He said, genuinely taken back, "What do you mean?"

Now I was feeling flustered and even more bewildered. "Why did you have to address it? Why couldn't we have just lived like how we were living, and that would have been it?"

Carder's mouth opened, stunned before he could formulate a response. "So, you wanted me not to say how I felt and just continue living the rest of my life, with you, in some odd silent agreement?"

I was submerged in baffled anger and spewed out whatever words came to mind. The logic filter is out the window.

"Lucy?"

"I don't know."

"Lucy,"

"I said I don't know! I'm obviously thrown off! Can't you see what you just threw at me-"

"Threw at you? Oh, I'm sorry, I'm sorry I just threw my true and deepest emotions to you, probably the sincerest thing I've ever felt in my life."

"Carder, you know what I mean. After what just happened with Jude and me-"

"Oh, wow," Carder's voice wasn't sarcastic as before; it sounded like he was having yet another realization, but one he was disappointed about. "You do love him. You love Sherlock."

I just stared at him.

Catching my breath, I had stood up a few minutes ago when things started to get heated.

We were standing a few feet apart from one another.

My best friend.

"What? How could you- I don't know what I feel. I'm, there's too much going on right now." My eyes shut for a moment halfway through my rambling, almost yelling-sounding sentence. When they opened, they witnessed a silent tear stream down Carder's face.

I felt my mouth was opened a little bit, still in a bundle of confusion and frustration. My eyes were fixated on the sink, and they refused to move for some reason, even as my ears heard Carder put on his shoes, grab his keys, and open the apartment door.

Maybe he said something.

Or perhaps he didn't.

But I heard the door shut, and it released my eyes from its trance at its echoing close.

To see that Carder, in fact, had left.

His feelings are hurt.

I hurt his feelings.

Carder's most genuine, most profound feelings.

He's in love with me,

in some unconventional platonic type way;

but still.

I looked into the kitchen sink, and to my surprise, our sturdy, beautiful plates now had some chips in them.

I grabbed the cup of coffee off the table, not that I thought I deserved it, but I most certainly felt like I needed it. I kept my composure until I made it to my room. Then felt the heat from the downpour of tears on my face. I didn't even have the energy or care to shut my bedroom door. What would be the point anyway?

Back in my room.

My simple room with my pathetic twin-sized bed, with my muddled thoughts.

How could so much just happen, and I hardly feel any control over it?

I just didn't know what to say.

How can someone be expected to give a well-thought response to such a surprise like that?

How do I even feel?

Do I like Jude?

I know I like him; even in the confusing events of today, he's been nothing but kind to me.

But was that all genuine?

Do I love Jude-

I don't know...

I know I love Carder.

But in the way he loves me?

I don't know, I guess, maybe?

Or maybe I just feel so comfortable with him, and it seems like I should love him that way.

I sat on the edge of my bed for a while with my cup of coffee. My thoughts ran in every direction they could possibly think of when I thought I heard the door open.

I wasn't totally sure what I heard was the door, so I didn't react or move until I heard steps coming down the hall.

I was so relieved that Carder came back so we could talk.

I felt so awful inside that he left.

Even though it'll be challenging, he's still my best friend, and I want to talk to him about what happened.

I need to talk to him.

I knew he couldn't have gone that far anyway; that wouldn't be like him.

"Carder, I-" I was about to apologize as I thought he was coming into my room, but I stopped abruptly. "Seth?"

22. The King of Hearts

"**Y**ou left the front door open, Mac. Not a very safe thing to do. You should always lock your door."

Carder must have left it unlocked when he left. He was pretty distracted, given he had just poured his heart out, and I practically glossed over it.

"Why haven't you been answering me? All I was trying to do was talk to you. This all could have been a lot different if you had just answered me and we talked."

Seth seemed eerily calm, and I was beyond freaked out. He looked like he hadn't slept in days. "You can't just walk in here; you need to leave."

"I *needed* to talk to you. That's what I've been *trying* to tell you."

"I can *refuse* to talk to you, and that's what I'm doing. I will call the cops. I do not need this right now. Get out!" Surprisingly, I spoke with authority and without fear as I stood up and pointed toward the exit.

But then, my stomach felt a deepened pit I never thought I'd feel as Seth's response was to point at me.

"Do not talk to me like that,"

Not with his hand.

"All I ever wanted to do was talk to you, work things out, continue to grow and know each other, love you, and keep *our* promise."

But with what he apparently brought with him, tucked in the back of his pants.

"I have had this planned and played in my head for quite some time now, and never did I think you'd talk to me like that, Mac."

Seth was standing by my bedroom door while I was sitting on the edge of my bed, trying not to tremble and erupt in panicked tears as he pointed a pistol at me.

I didn't even know if he knew how to use that thing, which added to my panic. I couldn't even grasp what was going on; what was happening?

"I don't-"My voice was shaking so bad. "I don't understand what's going on."

I was crying with my words.

I couldn't help it.

I had never been this close to a gun, let alone have it pointed at me.

"There's a lot you don't know," Unlike my voice, Seth's hand was steady. "Why don't you sit down."

I tried to calmly sit, but I was so scared I sat down super-fast, and my coffee spilled a little.

"Kind of sucks. I had to pull this out just to get you to listen and talk to me. But you always needed help listening, didn't you, Mac?"

I felt completely out of control now. All I could do was cry. But it didn't even sound like I was crying. Tears were streaming down, but it was as if I was entirely on mute.

"I've been waiting a long time. A long time to tell you everything I've done for you, for us. A long time of just waiting for you. And I always told myself you were worth waiting for, but you gradually became so ungrateful, and I didn't even know who you were anymore, Mac."

He could see the scared confusion on my face; he motioned me, with the pistol, to talk. "Before a little while ago, I hadn't seen you in like a year. I don't get what you're referring to?"

Seth abruptly chuckled. "Ah, that's the first thing you don't know, Mac. When I helped move you into this place, and you decided until after to tell me I couldn't stay with you and we were done, which was a shitty way to break up with me by the way, you thought I went on and moved to San Francisco like we had planned. But unlike you, I stay true to my plans and the things I promise. Just like you,"

I felt my eyes widen.

"I never left."

This was unbelievable.

"I thought eventually you'd come to your senses; you'd reach out to me, and we'd patch things up and find a way to break out of your lease or find a subleaser and move like we had planned. But it seemed like you were moving on."

Logically trying to follow along with all of these confessions, repainting my reality, and pretty much being in a hostage situation, I had never felt so utterly helpless.

"You got a new job, and you even went on a few dates, one of which was looking to get a little serious, so of course, I stepped in."

"Wait, what? You-" Memories flooded my current thoughts, trying to piece things together. The guy I had kissed and hung out with a few times, whose Grandparent was at the Nursing Home I worked for. Seth stopped him?

"Yes, Mac, I told him to get lost. Perhaps a little more persuasive than that, but that's the general gist of it."

I thought that guy blew me off, or I wasn't attractive to him. I had no idea it was because Seth scared the shit out of him or made a threat.

"Then Carder moved in with you, and that really set me off because he's a dick, and he's never supported our relationship. But I held off, and I waited patiently for you to realize your mistake of letting me go. But then, you started spending a considerable amount of time with this weirdo guy I had never seen before. He started coming over more often, you'd leave to go places with him, and you were smiling. You were smiling so much. And when I saw you were smiling wider than you had ever smiled with me, I knew I had to start taking matters into my own hands to help you realize it's you and I that belong together. Not you and someone else. That's when I pretended and posted on Facebook that I was 'back in town.' It partially worked in my favor that my Mom actually wasn't doing the best health-wise. She's better now, thanks for asking."

He's talking like a million miles an hour and with such pride and a matter-a-fact manner. I swear it's the scariest thing I have ever been in the presence of; I have no idea what he's thinking or doing or how I can get away.

"And the day at the coffee shop was no accidental run-in. I followed you there. I just waited to go in for a while, so you'd think I happened to run into you. And when you went to the restroom, it wasn't your fatal mistake to ask me to watch your things or that you left your phone on the table. It was that you never changed your passcode. Colin's birthday."

I felt disgusted by him saying Colin's name. Chill after chill ran down my spine at the fact that he followed me that day and all the other walks he must have followed me on for almost a year.

"I opened your phone, and it was opened to a conversation between you and this guy, I was assuming, given what the recent texts were about. And I quickly took pictures of your conversation with my phone, gathering the information I needed. That being his address and other interesting facts about him, like his deepest fear you conveniently just asked him before I came walking in. Bees, now that was not easy to swing." He laughed a little, admiring his own maniacal work, I can only assume.

I gasped in horror. "You're why Jude was hospitalized; you put the beehive in his car."

"Like I said, not easy to do. I thought after that he'd stay away from you or leave, but nope. After that, I posed as a person who lived nearby, 'running into him' on one of his walks. I must say, Mac, I'm a gifted actor. I played that guy so well; he was so desperate for friends that it was pretty easy to become one. We exchanged phone numbers; we went for walks every once in a while. Oh, I played it well. I did it so well, so incredibly clever. I stayed lowkey enough in his life that he wouldn't feel a need to mention me but checked in on him enough to know what you guys were doing, hence-"

"The New York trip, the slashed tires."

"Yes, exactly; I was excited to say that part. I wish you would have let me finish. And you!" His sudden exclamation made me jump. "You, my dear, are clever as well. You found my trademark, my signature. And I can't believe you actually left the town, the state." Seth's eyes gleamed for a moment but took on a much darker tone as he continued. "We were supposed to do that together, Mac. You and I, I was going to be the one to help you overcome that obstacle. That was supposed to be me. I was prepared to do that. Not some guy who hardly even knows you and some loser who came crawling to you when their life fell apart."

Petrified, I was trying to process it all. Like walking into a movie at its climax, and you've only got the trailer to go off of.

Seth interrupted my analogy. "You're putting it together correctly." His condescending voice rang through my ears.

I hate when he does that. When he thinks he's replying to precisely what's being shouted in my head. I hate it even more when he's spot on.

"The crumbled up, scrapped up, fucked up playing cards- those are from me. I put one under the beehive and another in the slashed tire you found. But you're not asking about the best part."

My eyes narrowed; I'd never seen him hysterical before. In fact, I've never seen anyone act this purely insane.

"Go ahead, *ask me*. The answer is very witty and just the perfect detail."

I could barely speak; I felt my hand quivering, and my heart was beating so loud I swear we could both hear it.

"Ask me!" Seth's voice roared, and his hand shook a little, the pistol unsteady for a moment.

Provoking a shriek out of fear and then following his command. "Why! Why the playing card? Why that card?" Like a child, I wanted so badly to hide under the covers of the quilt I was sitting on. I didn't want to know the answer. I didn't want any of this to be real.

He grinned with satisfaction. "I scrapped the back of the card off because there's only one of my desired card in each deck, and it just looked eerier. And as for the specific card," Seth's demeanor changed as if we reached the second half of a play and the character's motives have shifted, and you feel an inevitable ending coming. "Do you notice anything odd about this card?"

He pulled a card, just like the other two, out of his pocket and flicked it towards me as it harshly landed on the bed. It landed face up as I looked at it, examining it with foggy eyes. "It's, it's a King of Hearts." My shaky voice confirmed.

Seth nodded and cleared his throat, like a bored Professor waiting for his pupils to catch up. "Yes, King as in male, hearts as in love. What else do you see in the card?"

Looking back at it, I didn't notice anything until I looked closely at the King's face. And as my eyes focused, I felt my whole body clench. A gasp flew from my throat just before it clamped shut. This couldn't possibly be happening.

"Yes, Mac, you've got it. The sword is through his head. It's nicknamed, the suicide King."

23. Spilled Coffee 

I looked at him with disturbed eyes and shook my head. I kept shaking my head, still silently crying, trying to catch up with my nightmare-turned-reality. "Seth, please, what is happening?" It felt like a stupid question to ask, but there was nothing else that would come out of me. I sounded so desperate, so scared, so helpless. Entirely, I was.

To my astonishment, I heard the slightest sniffle from him and realized he had started crying too. Not in the same way I was, but tears nonetheless. "I've been sad for so long, Mac, and I just thought if we could be back together, it would fix everything. I would feel purpose again, and we would be happy again. But you didn't care about me anymore, even when I tried to come back."

My head kept shaking in disbelief like it was the only thing I was capable of doing. I couldn't get any words out besides the pleas that barely escaped my vocal cords. Maybe they were even too soft to be heard. Perhaps I'm not speaking at all, and it's just in my head; too petrified to speak.

"And I tried to come back for you, for us, to keep our promise."

"Seth, Seth, please," I gasped out in despair, watching his shaking hand.

"Our promise, Lucy. Do you remember our promise?"

"Plea-" I couldn't stop sobbing. My body felt frozen to the bed, my hand frozen to this cup of coffee. Would my whole life now be frozen at this moment?

"Lucy, dear, I'm getting a bit impatient."

I knew he was staring at me, waiting for me to answer and look at him. My chest had never felt tighter, and a few tears rushed down my face, contributing to it. With a shallow breath, I pushed out the answer he was looking for. The answer I knew immediately when he said the word promise. And the memory of romantically nieve high school kids mending such words together flashed through my mind every time I heard that word since that promise was made. "We, we promised,"

Seth cleared his throat, a clear sign of demanding my eye contact.

I forced myself to look up at him, his silent tears staining a face caked with so many memories. In the fastest bleak blink, I couldn't believe my heart had the audacity to remember the guy I once loved and how completely gutwrenching our paths have ground out. My empathy leaked into my words for a moment, "We promised we'd be together. Forever," but that compassion burned out before my sentence had ended. "No matter what." And it was replaced, once again, with fear.

"That's correct, Mac. Exactly right."

Was that all he wanted? For me to admit a promise, we had made when we were teenagers?

"But I can't live like this anymore, in this ache, this purposeless life."

A single thought of hope had planted itself in my mind before, hoping there would be some way out of this. That Seth would collapse and say he needed help. I'd have a chance to call the police. Or Carder would come through the door and save the day. But seeing the expression on Seth's face deepen into this dark horror, each of those possibilities dissolved. All but one; a sliver of hope that Carder would sense that something was wrong and he would get help.

Seth tapped his foot, bringing the room's attention back. "So, I came back one last time for you, for us both." More tears fell down his face. The hand holding the pistol was shaky with anxiety for a moment and then perfectly still the next as his words cut straight through me. "Lucy, why have the two people who have loved you most in this world do this to themselves? I'm just realizing this now."

My vision, within their human nature of protecting oneself, was concentrated on the gun but quickly turned to Seth's empty eyes in desperation. "Dd-done what?"

Within the moment my question was sent out to be answered, it remained untouched in the air between us.

It was instead interrupted by a loud piercing.

Seth's eyes stayed in my focus until I suddenly fell off my bed and now had a view of the floor and his shoes.

My ears were ringing.

I felt a shock surge through my body like I had never felt before.

I was wet,

my side was wet,

the side of my stomach is wet.

I can't describe what's happening to me,

the cold,

the shock,

the pain,

the confusion,

the-

Seth.

I saw Seth.

After another piercing ringing, I no longer saw his shoes but his face. His face was full of blood.

At first, I used to see a face full of laughter but then, later on, full of rage.

Drained of life when it used to be what I thought was the love of my life.

I could feel myself slipping.

From what I can't gather, I was still coherent enough to put together that Seth had shot me and then shot himself. I don't know if he meant to shoot me in the side, or if he missed, or if he intended on shooting just me or both of us. I couldn't bear to look at his face anymore, but I couldn't move any part of me. All I could do was avert my eyes, and even that felt like I was pulling all the strength I had in me. I could feel tears pouring down my face, falling into the horrible mixture of two different pools of blood on the floor. As my eyes tried to move to something else, I saw my coffee cup in its destroyed mess.

It had fallen when I did,

had broken like I did,

and was now spilling its contents just like me.

I stared at my coffee, which spilled out on the floor just inches away from me, just barely far enough to not be contaminated. This little puddle of coffee was my safe place right now. A sight away from the horrific reality in front of me. The fact that this may be my fate after all.

I loved my coffee.

I loved the smell of it.

I loved the simplicity of it.

I didn't hear the sound of it dropping on the floor.

And maybe it was just in my head, but I swear I can taste a little linger of its flavor from when I was sipping on it before Seth came into the room.

I couldn't tell how long I had been staring at it.

My eyes felt strained.

Like my vision was going in and out.

At times it felt like the lights in my room was getting brighter.

How long had they been doing that?

How long had I been on the floor?

How long had Seth been apparently dead?

How could any of this even happen? How could this have happened-

I heard something; am I hearing something?

Carder-

It must be Carder.

He's going to come in here and find me and take me to the hospital, and everything will be okay.

It took everything in me, every ounce of strength I had left, to pull my eyes away from the coffee, past Seth, and towards the door.

It had to be Carder.

It's always Carder.

It's always been Carder.

I couldn't move anything in me, lying helplessly on the ground, but I felt the corner of my lip turn just a tad as I saw him in the doorway. "Cc- Cc," My eyes were still adjusting to the random brightness going in and out of them, and as the light cleared, my struggling word changed and pushed through. "Colin?"

Epilogue

She said my name,

she's saying my name.

Right?

Yea, I can't make that up.

Usually, I tiptoe in her dreams when I think she needs a little guidance, or I'm just being selfish, and I miss her.

Have I always been selfish?

Lucy would say no.

What is she saying now?

I've never been summoned like this;

walking,

floating,

whatever it is I'm doing back in a plane I thought I'd never see again.

My vision is restored; it took a moment.

Dreams are typically fuzzy.

Lucy's on the floor.

That's her quilt, grandma's quilt.

And there's a cup of coffee; this must be her new room.

Spilled coffee-

Somethings wrong.

If I could just will this focus to sharpen–

Lucy's on the floor, hurt.

I can only think of one person who would commit such horridness; unfortunately, I'm correct.

Lucy can't be gone though.

Not her.

This can't be it.

I wish I could hold her; repay the kindness she gifted to me over and over again.

I could try?

Wait–

She's making a 'C-' sound again–

Can she see me in the bright hallway light?

Hallway light?

I don't remember that being on.

An intensity moved through me,

and now I see the figure of personified relief.

Perhaps Lucy really did see me at first, or she wanted me with her.

But it was Carder.

Isn't it always?

He's the best; I miss him.

I saw him shudder; a cold spot, he probably thought, but also at the sight of my sister.

I feel petrified; I'm ashamed.

I haven't done anything.

He's keeping her awake.

He's in shock.

He's phoning 911.

I can't physically do anything.

Yet, I won't get an opportunity like this again.

Maybe even just kneeling next to Carder and trying to place my hand on her will be enough?

I'll forever be in debt to the endless sincerity she graced me with, from start to finish.

Lucy's head slightly moved to mine and Carder's fascination.

Reactionarily, I looked at him, like we used to when something odd occurred.

His eyes stayed fixed on Lucy; he didn't see me.

But I can see his stubble, and the tired circled around his eyes; man, he's grown up.

Lucy's faint movement followed my hand as I placed it on her head.

She uttered my name in the form of a question.

Which made Carder's voice crack as he calmly corrected her.

He kindled this sudden alertness of hers while they waited for help.

My hand smoothly rubbed her hair as a particular sense of Deja Vu glazed harshly over me.

No, that's not Lucy's story.

Retreating my hand, I stayed close to her, but I didn't want to confuse her or persuade Lucy to come with me.

She belongs here.

Her story has to continue.

Stepping back granted me to see Carder fighting back tears and nausea at the sight of this scene.

And a polarizing flood of actions and emotions erupted the room as paramedics and police hastily approached.

One thing after another,

everything lept into action.

Words flew so fast.

Like the bullet that cleanly went through Lucy's side.

And the one that completed Seth's final task.

Was Carder her boyfriend?

Hesitation,

Correction–

Roommate.

Best friend.

He could come in the ambulance.

I was coming too.

Just until I know, Lucy is stable.

That she's okay.

She has to be okay.

The hospital feels as cold as me.

Or perhaps it's saturated with unpleasant memories.

With everything in me, I want to hold Lucy's hand.

Rushed down the fluorescent oasis.

But I don't want to accidentally pull her away.

Carder's hand slips into hers.

Running alongside the stretcher.

He tells her everything is going to be okay.

And that he loves her.

And he's sorry.

Of course he loves her,

why is he sorry?

Lucy says my name again, without question.

Before Carder can speak, he is pulled away by a nurse.

He isn't allowed in the room.

Sterilized.

Surgery.

Silence.

Hours pass.

It feels like an eternity for me.

I can't imagine what it feels like for Carder and their worried face friend.

Their new friend.

That's nice to see.

At first, there seemed to be some outside tension.

But that quickly dissolved into the waiting room chairs.

Did Lucy go through this too?

A doctor gets their attention.

Our attention.

Lucy is stable.

Stable.

She's tired, but awake.

Awake.

Following them into the room, she lights up.

It takes me more than a beat to understand and accept that she no longer sees me.

Maybe she still feels my presence.

I climbed into the bed with her and rest my head on her shoulder.

Hoping she feels warm and safe.

I'm here.

Carder, and now by name, Jude, are beaming at Lucy.

She clears her throat.

Speaking in a whisper, at first, and ending her sentence in confi-

dence.

She tells them she saw me.

Lucy said, "I saw Colin; he was with me."

I'm shocked,

I'm happy,

I'm relieved.

I'm relieved she can't see me anymore.

She's going to stay here.

Jude smiles and tells Lucy that's remarkable.

Speechless.

As I internally agree, she addresses him by another name.

Sherlock?

That's funny.

And confusing.

Carder's voice breaks, again, as I see tear after tear cascade
down.

He's overwhelmed.

He's happy.

She's alive,

she's okay.

We made sure she was okay.

Carder, thank you for picking up my slack.

A knock on the door alerts us all.

And I've seen plenty of movies and TV shows, so I know what a detective looks like.

Even more so when they've got a few burning questions.